DEAR DAUGHTER DEAD

S. B. HOUGH

DEAR DAUGHTER DEAD

S. B. HOUGH

PERENNIAL LIBRARY

Harper & Row, Publishers

New York, Cambridge, Philadelphia, San Francisco

London, Mexico City, São Paulo, Sydney

A hardcover edition of this book was published in England by Victor
Gollancz Ltd. in 1965, and in the United States by Walker & Co. in 1966.
It is here reprinted by arrangement.

First PERENNIAL LIBRARY edition published 1983.

Library of Congress Cataloging in Publication Data

Hough, S. B. (Stanley Bennett), 1917-
   Dear daughter dead.

   (Perennial library ; P/661)
   I. Title.
[PR6058.083D4   1983]   823'.914   83-47583
ISBN 0-06-080661-3 (pbk.)

83 84 85 86 87 10 9 8 7 6 5 4 3 2 1

CHAPTER ONE

Brentford descended to the shore at a time of day when he always felt he could have lived in a different way and that he should have done a different kind of work. The child's body was sprawled nakedly on the rocks by the creek, with one foot trailing in a pool of water, in an attitude that seemed to him to be indecent and obscene.

The impression was strengthened by the official and over-dressed male figures moving round it. Lent, who looked up as Brentford came down, was using his cameras to take a photographic survey. McIver watched and waited impatiently, holding his black bag. Uniformed policemen wandered around the scene, having no trouble with crowds or people, yet trying to look formal and impassive, as though they knew what they were doing.

They looked up at Brentford with relief. If he could not solve the problems, he could take responsibility for them. Crosston, in charge of the uniformed branch, came a little towards him. They all expected something, and Brentford, who knew that every case was different, tried not to show that he felt the familiar, early-morning sense of not knowing where to begin.

He nodded to Crosston, looked at the body which had been reported to him as that of a child, and saw that it was more like that of a young woman. "Get on with it, Lent," he said, seeing the photographer as the reason that the body was uncovered and the doctor delayed. He looked around at the uniformed men, glanced at the nakedness of the body, and said, "You're looking for the clothes?"

Two unoccupied policemen, walking the beach and searching the rocks and crevices, began to look more as though they knew what they were looking for. And Ball, his own man, had seen him and was coming up the grassy slope from the direction of the sandy shore.

To Brentford, the appearance of the Sergeant was the one reassuring factor of the case, establishing the accepted pattern. It was the beginning of routine.

Ball, as usual, had got there before him, presumably without his breakfast. Across the creek, the early morning sunlight was shimmering on the trees and on the gables of one of the half-hidden houses of the Trequayne Estate.

The Trequayne Estate was the nearest habitation. Ball looked as though he already had something to tell, but was not unduly hopeful about it, having already decided that it did not mean anything.

Brentford guessed. "Footprints?" he said to Ball.

"Only his," Ball said dryly, and jerked his head in the direction of the police car.

Brentford looked back up the grass and rock slope in the direction of the car. It was one of the three which, together with the ambulance, were drawn up on the curve of the road where it came down over the hill from Loebeach village. There was an old man sitting in the seat beside the driver's in the first car.

"He found her?"

Brentford did not have to begin. The thing began itself. It was always like that.

Ball made his report of what he had discovered, of the situation on his arrival. In doing so, he glanced at Crosston and the other men of the uniformed branch, whom he had got it from. They could listen if they wished, and check the details.

"He's called Martin." Ball indicated the old man. "He collects wood along the beach here in the mornings. The tide was out. He was finished and about to turn back. It was chance he saw the body. She was further up the creek than he would look for driftwood. When he saw her, he began to go up the slope to go back to Loebeach. Then he went down to have a look. Then he ran up the hill. He says he ran all the way up the hill to Loebeach. He's sixty-five."

Brentford registered something. Something about the body

being in a position farther up the creek than driftwood would drift. It might not be important.

"What happened then?"

"He called at the first house. You can see it, the roof of the bungalow on the hill above Loebeach, overlooking the river. They asked him why he didn't go to the Trequayne Estate which was nearer. He said the Trequayne Estate was private. Instead, he ran all the way up the hill and rang the doorbell of the first house. They weren't up, and when he didn't get an answer at once, he didn't wait. He ran out again, and all the way down into Loebeach to the public call box. The desk sergeant told him to wait where he was. They sent a patrol car to pick him up. They brought him back here, and he showed them the body."

Brentford found nothing remarkable in any of that. He added up the times. Up the hill from the small creek, an old man following the curving road, then down into Loebeach with its inn and hotel and dracaena-palm gardens looking out across the bay. The public phone was between the hotel and the gardens. Say half an hour. He himself had got the call when the phone rang while he was finishing breakfast at home at seven-thirty. Martin must have been beachcombing along the tidemark before six a.m. Perhaps you had to be as early as that if you wanted to be the first to get anything that drifted in with the night tide.

"You say he was turning back? She was farther up the creek than he would have expected anything to drift?"

Ball looked back at him. "You mean the body was put in the creek here?" His voice was wary.

It was an inference that Ball himself could make, but it had not been Ball's business to make inferences when reporting facts.

Ball did not want to make inferences on vitally important matters so early in the case. He might allow himself liberties later, but it was up to Brentford to say when inferences were accepted, so that they became facts.

"We'll see," Brentford said.

Since Ball had finished his report, he turned to the body. If he accepted the inference that "the body had been put into the

7

creek," he would be making not one inference but two. The second would be that the body had been dead when it went into the water. He could not assume that.

Such considerations had to be delayed until the body had been examined, and that was a distressing business. They might have to be delayed until they got the medical report later.

Brentford moved away from Ball and towards the body. He left the grass and picked his way across the rocks. The photographer, finding Brentford suddenly appear in a picture he had been about to take, desisted.

McIver, the doctor, seeing his opportunity, moved in with Brentford. They did not touch anything at that stage, but stood looking, standing near the high-tide mark on the rocks just above the body.

There was a frightful clarity about the sight.

The body was bent backwards. The foot that was trailing in the water, in the pool between the rocks, looked as though it had grounded and wedged, leaving the body to settle and take up its position as the tide went out. The hair was fair, matted and sea-drenched, and trailing down the other side of a rock as though it had still been floating in the ripples when the tide had left the torso. The head was thrown back, the mouth was open, and the tongue protruding. The eyes were staring. The arms were evidently fixed and rigid. The girl had been fifteen or sixteen years old, and might have been pretty, and must certainly have been striking with that hair, but it was hard to tell if she had been beautiful now, with that expression on her face.

McIver settled one of the questions in Brentford's mind. "Rigor mortis before she settled here," he said.

It became a question of the tides. It was always something. Brentford too made his direct assumptions:

"Will you be able to tell me how long ago she was strangled, before she went into the water?"

He and the Doctor looked at the marks on the throat.

"You know the difficulty. It doesn't look on the face of it as though I shall find water in the lungs to indicate she was breathing when she went in."

"Poor kid," said Ball, who had come to stand beside them.

Brentford said nothing to that. Even Ball should not have said it. It was one of the things that went too far beyond saying.

Brentford frowned at the body and frowned at the public road leading back up the hill to Loebeach. In the other direction, the road led to the Trequayne Estate. He had a good view of the road from by the body, and that meant that the body could be seen from the road; and the photographer with his tripod had not yet finished.

"We are holding up proceedings," he said.

As he moved back, Crosston came to join them.

Brentford moved him back from the body.

"I closed the road," Crosston said to Brentford. "It means that the people in the Trequayne Estate will be cut off for a while, but we can't help that." He sounded hard.

Brentford looked beyond the body and across the creek to the Trequayne Estate, then back at the body.

"I want to work on her where she is for a while," McIver said. "It's the best way to answer the question you asked me."

Brentford jerked his shoulders impatiently.

"Has she been in the mud?" he asked McIver. "Or is she naturally that colour?" He made his first observation.

Unbidden, everyone stared at the body, trying to deduce something from the pallor of the corpse.

Except that it was not a completely white pallor.

McIver glanced at the photographer again and went forward. He had to place himself awkwardly on the rocks. Without moving the corpse, he rubbed the skin of the thigh and hip with his finger.

He looked up at Brentford and shook his head. Whatever it was, it did not come off.

"Sunburn," he said.

Brentford jerked his head upwards and stalked away. Behind him, the little crowd broke up. The photographer was able to complete his work before the doctor could conduct his preliminary examination in greater detail. Brentford walked up the slope a little.

9

When he got there, he swung around and looked across the creek at the woods and the two visible houses of the Trequayne Estate. He turned left to look at the little bridge at the head of the creek, then he turned right again to look at the mouth of the creek, where it joined the bay with the river. From the point of the land between the creek and the river, the beaches led back to Loebeach. Loebeach could be where the girl had come from.

But he looked back at the good houses in the woods on the private land of the Trequayne Estate.

"You're right, Inspector," Ball said, having come to stand near him and await his orders. "That girl is more sunburned in more places than she would ever get to be on a public beach."

Then he too looked at the Trequayne Estate, but it was just a guess, and anyone could guess. The difficulty was to know.

CHAPTER TWO

Check, Brentford thought. Don't leap to conclusions. About vital facts, check and check again.

He looked at the police cars. Another was arriving, with a squad of men. Crosston would have asked for it, from headquarters by radio. Crosston would need a lot of men. He knew he was not going to find the clothes so easily.

Down in the creek, away out towards the river, and where there was a pool of deeper water even at low tide, there was a small yacht. It was not near the body, and it seemed unlikely that it had anything to do with it.

"Take a walk along the beach and see if there's anyone aboard that craft," he said to Ball.

Ball looked at the yacht. There was no dinghy trailing astern of it, but there was a light little pram-tender on the cabin roof. "I will," he said. He took a uniformed man and went off along the beach, receding.

If there was anyone aboard the yacht, they would have had a view up the creek during the night, if they had looked out, but it was a large if.

Brentford turned and went to Crosston, who was dispersing his men not only along the beach but across the grass slopes. A murderer might put clothes anywhere. Sometimes, in such situations, he took them away in a car.

"Have headquarters reported anyone missing, answering to the description?" Brentford said formally.

"All of you," Crosston was saying to his men. "Methodically. We don't want to have to go over this ground again."

He left them and turned to Brentford.

"Not yet," he said flatly.

"She must have been missing from her home since last night," said Brentford.

"Headquarters are going through the list of missing persons," Crosston said. "The nearest so far is a girl missing in London six weeks ago. The description isn't right, but they're going to check."

Headquarters were right, Brentford thought. No one was more mobile than under-age girls on their way to being murdered. She could have come from anywhere in the country, or out of it. He should not overlook that even though he found himself not believing it. The girl was sunburned.

"You have men at Loebeach checking through the village?"

"Yes, but the news will be through the village since we closed the road. If any girl had been missing the parents would have come forward."

Brentford turned and watched Ball and the constable. They had walked up the beach and were standing on the shore and calling "Yacht ahoy!" Their calls were distant.

Even if there was anyone aboard the yacht, it was unlikely they would have looked out at the right time. If the murderer was aboard the yacht, he would not have stayed there. He would have pulled up anchor and sailed away.

"Ahoy! Were there any more yachts here last night?"

"No! What is——? I say!" The answer came faintly.

A young man came out on deck and stood staring towards Brentford and the police. A female head came up, revealing a bare pair of shoulders which promptly ducked down again as soon as their owner saw the activity on the shore. Brentford registered the presence of the girl with depression. If the young man had been alone, he would have spent the evening looking out. With a young woman aboard his boat, he would have had other things to think about. That was the way it went. People did not spend a lot of time looking out for other people, and Brentford did not expect it.

He continued his business with Crosston, glancing to the nearer distance across the creek.

"What about the Trequayne Estate?" he asked.

Crosston looked towards the body and tried to express something: "Do you think their daughters would be the kind to get themselves involved like that with a man?" He made presumptions.

"Have they got any daughters?"

"I don't know."

It all had to be done, speculation and elimination of possibilities. Meanwhile Brentford imagined the murderer getting further from the spot or covering his tracks. It was a disaster that it always happened like that, but it did.

Ball, on whom Brentford depended to make his next move, was now involved with the irrelevant yachtsman. The young man had put his little pram dinghy over the side and was rowing urgently to the shore. Crosston's men were making slow progress. One of them had reached the head of the creek, crossed the little bridge, and was beginning to work his way back on the other bank. Brentford kept a sharp eye on his progress. He was as interested in the farther shore as in the near one. He tried to be interested in everything.

"I'll find out if the Trequayne people have any daughters," Crosston said, beginning to move.

"Don't worry. I may go there myself," Brentford said, looking at the man on the farther bank.

Crosston stood and stared at him. He found Brentford's statement unexpected, a leaping to conclusions.

There was nothing actually except proximity to tie the murdered girl with the beautiful houses still sleeping in the morning sunlight on the far bank of the creek, secure in the expensive privacy of the estate. No one from there had reported any daughters or young girls missing, but then they had not reported anything else, either, not even a complaint about the road being closed, and they were probably not yet up.

Looking at the roofs among the leaves in the golden sunlight of the beautiful morning, Brentford said: "They are the nearest habitations. We will have to make inquiries."

Crosston looked dubious. McIver came up to them.

"Death was due to strangulation, prior to immersion. That is still a guess."

Brentford kept an eye on everything. Ball was leaving the yachtsman and was coming back. By the body on the rocks, two ambulance men were standing with a stretcher but were not doing anything.

"What's the hold-up?" he asked McIver.

"I want to do some more work on the body, and be with it when they move it. If any fluid comes out, it is important I should know what it is. But I came to you because I thought you would want a preliminary report on superficial wounds."

Brentford tensed. He became quickly expectant.

He knew what McIver meant when he spoke of superficial wounds in connection with the body of a murdered girl. In one sense, this was it.

"Are there any, apart from the strangulation at the neck?"

McIver met his eye. "She has scratches on the outside of the legs, as though she was running through brambles. But that is all that is definite."

McIver could not commit himself to what a post-mortem would show, but he was being significant.

Crosston looked around the hillside on their side of the creek for brambles, to direct his men to them. There were none. The side of the creek with the road was grass and rock. It was the other side that had woods and brambles.

Brentford looked as though he were making up his mind. At the same time he continued to look expectantly at McIver, as though the doctor had not quite come to the point.

"No bruising of the breasts, thighs or inner side of the legs," said McIver, his voice deliberate.

13

Crosston too switched his gaze sharply to McIver.

"The first thing the Super will want to know is whether this is a sex-crime that is likely to be repeated," he said. He was not satisfied with negatives.

"I can't tell you whether she was raped," McIver said. "I can only tell you what I have not seen. Because there is no superficial evidence, I shall have to tell you later whether she was a virgin or if intercourse took place."

"The Super won't be happy," Crosston said.

McIver coloured slightly. "You want it both ways," he said. "I take the trouble to tell you what I have found right away, and you want me to give you my final word."

"That's all right, Peter," Brentford said, quickly.

Later, when the doctor had gone, he spoke to Crosston. "You shouldn't have said that to McIver, Arthur."

Brentford too would incur the Super's displeasure for not knowing what kind of a crime it was, but it was only one of the innumerable things he did not know, and he had to keep the team working smoothly. It was one part of his work.

"The yachtsman didn't want to give his girl's name," Ball said, arriving. "Apart from that, he saw nothing."

Brentford looked impatient. "You got the names?"

"Fred Harding and Miss Alice Sillitoe. That is if he did not invent her name. I asked him about tides."

Brentford's gaze became expectant, more patient.

"There was no wind last night," Ball said. "He knows this place well. Perhaps this is not the first girl he has brought here. When he throws empty bottles and potato peelings over the side, they circle round. They don't drift straight out to sea on the ebb as you would expect, but stay as an ugly sight in the creek."

Ball pointed. There was an old quay and a boat aground across the mud and water. He spoke deliberately of the rubbish.

"They drift to the far bank there and then come back before they reach the bridge. He finds items he has discarded on this side, near where he lands in the dinghy to go to Loebeach. It isn't very good evidence. He isn't very clear. But at least he knows the times of the tides. He says the body would have to be put in the water about midnight to end up where it is. Naturally he wasn't looking out, and he was too far away to hear anything."

Brentford listened intently and with concentration. It might be something, and it might be nothing. It was only later that evidence would prove to be important.

Then he had to decide on his next move.

"You and I will interview the owners of the houses," he said. He looked back towards Loebeach, but rejected it, and looked across the creek.

"We will?" Ball said.

Someone had to interview the occupiers of all the nearby properties, but Ball had assumed that he would do it, as he had in the case of the yachtsman, or that reinforcements and a squad of detectives would be called for.

"What are the chances that the girl comes from the estate?" Brentford said. "If she doesn't, we will soon give up and look elsewhere."

It was not that which worried Ball.

"What about setting up a local headquarters?" he said.

The correct thing for Brentford to do, if he followed the copy-book pattern of how to conduct a murder case, was to take over a schoolroom or village hall at Loebeach, make it his headquarters and bring in a secretary and a typewriter. From that position, he would direct the murder hunt and devote himself to reading reports and administration until a definite picture emerged and there was something specific for him to do.

He showed no resentment of his sergeant's hint as to what would be regarded as the correct conduct of the case, nor did he say anything about the particular brutality of the crime. So far as appearances went, he was unaffected.

He spoke to Ball in a casual, less-than-formal way.

"Fifty per cent of murderers remain undetected," he said mildly. "A corpse always looks so dead, and so do detectives' reports and typed sheets of interviews. What I would prefer to do would be to treat it as though the girl were still alive."

They were walking away up the slope towards Crosston, and

Ball made no attempt to try to look as though he had understood what Brentford had said.

"If just by any chance she did come from the estate," Brentford said, "and if the situation is still alive——"

They reached Crosston, to whom Brentford did not attempt to explain himself. "I am going on to the estate to take a look at that quay over there," he said to the uniformed inspector.

"Where do I tell the Superintendent that your headquarters will be?" said Crosston. He was no slower than Ball to remind Brentford of what he should be doing.

"Tell him I will keep in touch with him by way of the radio in the car for the time being," Brentford said. "If he asks you, that is. Otherwise, don't say anything."

CHAPTER THREE

It was very little later that the car crossed the little bridge and stopped at the lodge-gate.

Moodily, Brentford watched Ball go to open the gate so that the driver could take the car through. There was a notice on the gate that said "Private". Brentford wondered if the whole peninsula was private, between the creek and the sea, and what kind of a place it was.

There was a movement by the old cottage or lodge just inside the gate, and an old man came out and spoke to Ball as he opened the gate, checking a dog that came with him.

"You can't come in here," he said, obliviously.

Brentford wondered if that were useful information, implying that the news of the murder had not penetrated to the estate as yet. The man's attitude seemed genuine.

Through the windscreen, Brentford watched Ball and the old man.

"Police," Ball said.

"You can't come in here," the old man said.

"We must," said Ball.

"I don't care if you are the police," the old man said. He looked shrewd and obstinate. "You can't come in here without a warrant." Clearly, he knew nothing of murder.

Legally, Brentford thought, the old man was probably stating the truth, if only to be awkward. It told him something about the Trequayne Estate.

Having fixed the gate, Ball turned to the old man. "Do many people come in and out this way?" he asked.

"Only residents," the old man said.

"Did anyone come in or out last night?"

"The residents didn't, and I wouldn't let anyone else." The old man looked at his dog, grinning anciently.

"Who owns the old quay with a boat tied to it, along the shore?" said Ball.

The old man looked at him suspiciously. "Mr. Morris," he said. "Is he the one you want to see?"

"He is the one we've got to see," Ball said.

Coming back and getting into the car again, he spoke to Brentford.

"Closing the road may have been more useful than we thought."

They drove through the gateway on to a gravel drive, which ran up through the woods, branching to the new houses. Brentford looked out of the window at the cottage as they passed it.

"No telephone at the lodge," he said. "The houses will have them."

They would not necessarily be ahead of the news, despite the old man.

The silent driver spoke for the first time, a man with the rank of constable, who only drove the car.

"If whoever lives here murdered the kid," he said, "I don't care if he's Lord Trequayne himself."

"There is no Lord Trequayne any more," Brentford said, looking at the desecrated but still private woods.

Judging by the rhododendron bushes, the initial drive they were following must have once run to the big house, which, like the old Lord Trequayne, was no more. New drives had been cut off it however, and they came to a junction.

"You want me to try this one for the house with the quay, sir?" the driver said. It was impossible to see the exact locations of the new buildings now that they were in the woods. It was a big estate, even the portion of it that had been sold off for building, and the new inhabitants must have spent considerable sums. The driver was finding the circumstances unusual and was having difficulty locating the particular house they wanted.

"Try it," Brentford said with no great concern. It was a house by the shore he wanted. He did not know which one.

Meanwhile they were in woodland which was unfortunate in that it was big enough for a dozen murders simultaneously. It would take an army of men to search it if the body could be connected with the Trequayne side of the creek.

Brentford tried to think of any items of information that had led him to place the body as belonging to that side. They were small: the fact that the girl was sunburned as though she had had a private place to sunbathe, the scratches on the legs of the body, and the yachtsman's evidence about the tides. None of them was conclusive. None were such that he would take pleasure in explaining to the Super what had led him to abandon normal procedures.

None of them was such as to give him a line of inquiry and questioning when he came to the owners of the houses. He could not inquire about anything specific, but only put such questions as "Do you have a daughter who is missing?" and "Did you hear or see anything unusual last night?" Those were the kind of questions that he could command a squad of constables to put to householders.

There was no fence or wall when they came in sight of the first house. The landscape was unusual.

The wall they had passed at the gate cut off the estate as a whole. Within the estate, the inhabitants could apparently trust one another sufficiently to leave the woods in a virtually unspoiled state, without heavily marking the boundaries of their properties. So there was no abrupt transition from woods to garden. The area of felled trees and flower-beds extended into the woods at will, apparently as far as the owner had money and energy enough to extend them, and the house stood in the middle of them.

It was a very modern structure, consisting largely of glass apparently, and highly suited to the privacy of its situation. Yet despite its modernity, it did not look unfitting. As they approached cautiously down the now descending drive towards the creek, Ball said:

"Do you think they had an architect design the house for the situation, or do you think they had the house first and got God to design the landscape round it?"

Brentford grunted. Somehow he did not think that the people in that particular house had lost a daughter. If they had, he imagined from their social position, they would probably have been in a position to communicate direct to the Home Office about it.

Either they were people like that or they had made an extraordinarily shrewd real-estate deal.

"Which is the front door?" the driver said, finding it difficult to know where to stop the car opposite the many panes of glass.

CHAPTER FOUR

Not everyone kept the same hours as police and murderers.

They could see a woman through the glass. Visibly, she had just got up. She was wearing a dressing-gown and was not in a state to appear in public.

"May be a servant," Ball said.

"She'd be dressed if she were," Brentford said. Somehow, he did not see people keeping servants in a situation where loneliness was a consequence of the privacy.

They were standing at what they took to be the front door. It might alternatively have been the garden door. There was evidence that the panes of glass would open.

The interior of the house was directly visible. To the right was a kind of open space with low furniture, divided off from the rest by an indoor trellis with climbing plants. The woman was behind the trellis and low barriers in a functional modern kitchen. They watched her until it became clear that she had not heard Brentford when he had gently knocked.

It added to the conclusion that she had just got up and was not registering extraneous sounds very well as yet.

She was not registering anything very well. Clouds of steam arose from whatever she was doing. If she had been making coffee, she had just let it boil over.

They watched fascinated, for, despite the morning disaster, her temperament seemed equable and serene. She went on with what she was doing without any sign of irritation.

Brentford slapped the glass instead of knocking. It made a louder sound.

She turned and looked at them with acute surprise and mild dismay. Evidently she had not anticipated that anyone could penetrate the defences and reach the transparent house at that hour of the morning.

But she was not put out by their appearance. She took the two coffee cups that she had been preparing, departed to a screened-off portion of the house that was evidently the bedroom area, and ignored them.

Brentford could not feel that that, whatever else it was, was the conduct of a murderer. Also it left him in doubt whether to knock again or not. The woman had clearly seen them.

A man appeared. He too was in a dressing-gown. He brought one of the coffee cups with him, not intending to be separated from it no matter who was at the door. He came to the door and pressed a catch and the door opened.

It was up to Brentford then. He said: "Mr. Morris?" and looked expectant.

Morris, if that was his name, looked of middle age, between forty-five and fifty. He was a thick, heavy man, who looked as though he ate and drank and lived too well to be in the best of condition. None the less, he was still powerful, and showed a hint of character.

"What do you want? What business have you here?"

"We are the police."

Brentford watched carefully, as always, for evidence of a guilty reaction. It usually happened, even when the people were innocent of the crime being investigated.

Most people were guilty of something, if only of parking a car in a no-parking area three weeks ago.

Morris viewed them cautiously. It seemed unlikely that he had anything very serious on his conscience.

"Why have you come here?" he said.

He certainly did not welcome a visit from the police.

Nor did he look like a householder who had put a body in the creek from the quay below his house. But Brentford had already looked at that, at the house and the way down to the quay. If anyone else had taken a body there, it could not be taken for granted that Morris would have heard or noticed anything.

There was just a general probability in that direction.

Brentford offered the first official question that came into his head.

"You own a boat, Mr. Morris?" Then he improved on it. The police were presumed to be clear and definite. "You are Mr. Morris?"

The combination of questions sounded more than he intended.

From inside the house, from the bedroom that was at least sufficiently divided from the rest of the space to render the occupant invisible, the woman's voice called: "Who is it?"

Morris reacted to her rather than Brentford. In a voice that conveyed a minor, careful warning, he said: "It's the police." Perhaps he thought the warning was too strong. He said: "Something about the boat." Then he tried to cover all that to Brentford by saying: "Do you want to come in?"

On due consideration, Brentford decided to go in.

Morris led them into the big combined living room and sun-lounge. He evidently wondered why he had asked them in when he had got so far. He said: "What about the boat?"

Brentford was not completely satisfied with the very minor indications. He said, "Could we have your full name, sir?"

Morris stopped and looked at him and wondered more, as

21

he was bound to do. In answer, bluntly, he said: "Who are you?"

"Chief Detective Inspector Brentford and Detective Sergeant Ball," said Brentford.

Morris looked for a moment as though he did not believe it.

Then he said, "William Morris."

They sat down. Brentford asked the few questions he was able to ask. Socially he said, "Have you been here long, Mr. Morris?"

"About five years," said Morris dryly. He looked from Brentford to Ball, who had taken out a notebook, and said, fairly calmly: "What is all this?"

He had a right to know something, Brentford realised.

"Long enough, sir, to know if you heard anything or saw anything unusual last night," he said.

Morris said: "Should I? Last night?"

It looked a little beyond good acting.

The woman came in, or rather out of the secluded part of the house, which made her available immediately for conversation. It was an advantage or disadvantage of an open plan house that it was impossible to have private talks separately.

"What is it?" she said.

Morris said: "They have sent a Chief Detective Inspector and a Detective Sergeant to interview us about the boat."

Brentford did not blame him for his disbelief.

She was mildly concerned and came into the living-room compartment. "What for?" she said.

"Ask them," said Morris.

"Would you think carefully, Mr. Morris, and tell us if you heard or saw anything unusual last night?" Brentford said.

"I don't think so," said Morris. He looked at the woman and said: "Did you, while I was out?"

She thought, and said: "No."

Ball, with his notebook, taking down formal details, said: "Can I have your full name, Madam?"

She looked at him a little sharply, and said: "Betty."

Brentford looked at the house and the two people, and said: "Betty Morris, Madam?"

She hesitated before she said "Yes."

Brentford said: "This may be serious, Madam. It may entail giving your name in court."

She looked puzzled rather than frightened.

"Betty is known here as 'Mrs. Morris'," Morris said.

Another of them, Brentford thought. On a more permanent scale. It was fairly usual, in some places.

"We had better have your proper name," he said. "We don't broadcast these things unless it is necessary."

"Betty Keen," she said. "Betty, not Elizabeth." She seemed more concerned about that than the fact that she was not married.

Brentford turned to the one point he had established.

"So you were out at one time last night, Mr. Morris?"

Morris frowned. It was something he did not like.

"Not for long."

"At what time?"

"Around eleven or after."

"Doing what?"

Betty Keen laughed abruptly.

Morris went red and looked at her. Then he looked at Brentford but spoke as though in defiance of her:

"I won't answer that."

Brentford sat equably in his chair. "This is an important matter, sir," he said.

Morris said: "In what way important? What has it got to do with us?"

"A girl has died," Brentford said, and watched him.

Morris registered nothing.

Betty Keen frowned and looked a shade concerned and said: "What girl?"

Brentford looked steadily at her and said: "Do you know which girl it might be?"

She said nothing, looking puzzled. But he did not like her silence.

"Do you?" he said.

She said: "How should I know?" She seemed to mean it.

Brentford turned to Morris again. It all took far too long. He had a feeling that it should not take so long. But then he was always chiding detective sergeants like Ball with taking too long over establishing irrelevant matters and formal details.

"Now sir, please. Just when and where were you last night, and what were you doing?"

After a moment's consideration, Morris said : "I won't tell you, at least at present, and I don't see why I should. I don't understand this."

He had become antagonistic, as people did in answer to the wrong approach. He expected to be told the whole story to begin with. If you told people the whole story to begin with, they knew what your questions meant and coloured their answers accordingly.

Oh well, thought Brentford, perhaps I am out of practice in doing this. Perhaps Ball would have done it better.

Or if it had not been an open-plan house on an important estate, he thought, and he had been able to interview the people separately, which might be a good idea, if he had the time.

He surprised Ball.

"Very well, sir," he said. "And now, with your permission, we will go down and look at your quay and boat, and see what access there is from your garden into the creek."

He realised quite well that that probably meant a delay and more time, and that it had probably not been a good idea to set out to make these interviews personally.

CHAPTER FIVE

He felt it more strongly as they went down to the creek.

I am out on a limb, Brentford thought. I should never have used my time to come on a wild-goose chase like this. It is not that a detective-constable or a detective-sergeant could have done it as well; they could probably have done it better. I should be at Loebeach, comfortably reading their reports in the school-hall.

He was following Morris down the steep wooded path from the house to the quay, with Betty Keen following and Ball bringing up the rear.

Morris had thawed sufficiently to say he would show them the quay and the boat if they would give him a moment to put on some clothes. Brentford wanted that now, but he inferred that though it did not necessarily imply guilt, Morris wanted to keep them under observation, and Betty Keen to indulge a natural curiosity.

"Is this a murder case?" Morris said suddenly.

They were descending towards the creek, and from the narrow muddy path they had a view through the leaves over the mud and water. On the far, public bank of the creek, the grass slopes were thick with police who were searching for the missing clothes.

"Yes," said Brentford, looking at the path on which they were walking, which held footprints, despite the dry weather, where it was still damp beneath the trees. He tapped Morris on the back, stopped him, and went ahead.

"You didn't say the girl had been murdered!" Betty Keen said accusingly.

"Just stay where you are a moment please," said Brentford.

He looked at the path. They could see the quay ahead now. He could also see the way rocks shelved and the brambles and bushes formed a tangle above the beach at all other places except at the descent towards the quay. If the body had been launched into the water from the Trequayne Estate side, and if, as the doctor might confirm, it was dead some time before it reached the water, then the route to the quay was the most likely way for it to have been carried.

There were a lot of ifs. If Brentford were to follow his policy of looking for the clear and fresh and simple indications first, he had to take risks. Ratiocination, the elimination of possibilities and the tracing of the movements of everyone in the district, was something to do in a quiet headquarters somewhere.

"How many police have you got?" said Morris "Is this a sex-crime?"

I wish I knew the answer to that, Brentford thought.

He looked at the footprints in the mud of the path before them. An Indian tracker might have made sense of the pattern, but not Brentford. So far as he could see, men's and women's footprints were intermingled. Probably a woman's, or a man's wearing long slim shoes, were the most recent. He looked at the shoes his party were wearing. Betty Keen was wearing flat-heeled gardening shoes, and Morris stout, broad brown ones. He was going to have difficulty convicting them or anyone else on the evidence of the path.

"Step off on to the grass," he told them. "It's not necessary for you to come down, Miss Keen. If you can avoid the brambles without stepping on the path, Mr. Morris, I will be obliged if you will come with me."

"I will be obliged if you will call Betty either Betty or Mrs. Morris, Inspector," Morris said.

They all went down the slope, edging past the brambles. Ball considered it his duty to accompany the Inspector, and Betty Keen, after pausing, decided she did not want to be left behind.

If they could all get down to the quay without stepping on the path, so could the murderer, Brentford thought.

Assuming he was the kind of murderer who thought of such things, which the murderers of young girls usually were not.

"Someone has been at the boat," Morris said with surprise, noticing heavy footprints along the beach and looking at the position of the oars.

Brentford could see they had. But it was almost certainly one of Crosston's constables, the one he had seen working along the far bank of the creek looking for the clothes.

"You normally leave the boat here?" Brentford said, standing on the quay.

"Tied with a clove hitch, not a turn and two half hitches," said Morris promptly.

The old ring on the quay, to which the boat's painter was tied, bore its evidence clearly.

"Who else uses the boat, beside yourselves?"

"Everyone."

"What do you mean by everyone?"

26

"Everyone on the estate."

"Who is that?"

"The Silcrest family. The Trueman-Davieses. David Feltham."

"But it is your boat?"

"Of course it is our boat."

"But you let everyone use it?"

"That's the way we run this estate, Inspector. David Feltham owns the sea beach on the other side, but he lets us use it. It's in the title deeds, I think. At least we always assumed it was."

Brentford took a look backward into the woods. He could not see anything of the estate through the trees, least of all the dwellings, houses or bungalows of the other people who had been mentioned, but he tried to visualise an estate in which the wealthy practised some primitive kind of communism.

Put such an estate in one of the most beautiful parts of the English countryside, and it sounded like some kind of Utopia. He wondered why he had a kind of mental predeliction to think that utopias led to murder.

Pure prejudice, he thought.

"Shall I take a look at the boat?" said Ball.

Brentford raised no objection. It was highly likely that the searching constable had destroyed whatever evidence there had been, but pending the discovery of the clothes or the revelation of the identity of the girl, the question of just how and where she was put into the water was the best project they had to work on. Ball slipped down the mossy, unstable rocks of the quay and into the boat.

Watching him, Brentford thought that that would be difficult for anyone carrying a body. But then he realised that at midnight or one a.m. it would not be necessary. The tide would be up and the boat floating conveniently by the quay.

For that matter, unless someone was being exceptionally careful, it would not be necessary to use the boat at all. Just slide the body into the water, turn it in the direction of midstream, and give it a push. Especially if whoever it was was under the impression that anything pushed out into mid-creek would go out to sea with the tide, and not just circle round and land on the farther shore.

27

"What happens to the boat if it breaks loose?" he said to Morris.

"It drifts away up the creek to the bridge with the wind that broke it loose," said Morris.

Probably other people were better than he at inventing questions to test what people did and didn't know, thought Brentford.

"One oar wet," said Ball, standing uncertainly in the rocking boat and moving things gingerly.

"Dew," said Morris. "Most things are always wet here, until the sun gets on them."

"Lick the oar and see if it tastes salt," said Betty Keen with inspiration, but quietly. She could have meant it.

Ball looked at her but did not express himself. He turned back on the other oar.

"Dry on one side," he said.

That was a problem posing enough permutations and combinations of possibilities to occupy a football pool addict for a happy month, thought Brentford. Assuming that the constable who had moved the oars had turned one over, and that the sun had been drying them, it meant one thing. But equally someone could have used one oar only, as a scull or paddle.

A sound from the direction of the path to the house made them all turn round.

It was Brentford's driver, coming down the path in apparent haste and slipping in the mud which they had all been so careful to avoid during their own descent.

Brentford was not happy to see him. It was not so much a matter of the footprints, the evidence of which, if any, was in process of being destroyed in the rapid descent. More important was the fact that the driver had been left to keep in touch with headquarters by means of the radio in his car.

It might be good news, Brentford thought, on first seeing the man. One of Crosston's men might have found the clothes, together with such incriminating evidence as would make it important to get in touch with Brentford urgently. But somehow Brentford had no faith in that. The man did not look as though he were bringing a pleasant message. He looked worried.

28

It seemed more likely that the driver was bringing a message from the Superintendent, demanding a progress report and asking where Brentford's local headquarters was. And just how, Brentford wondered, was he to prove, even to himself, far less to the Superintendent, that he was not wasting time?

"Mind the path!" Betty Keen called up to the driver.

The driver stopped and stared at them.

"The path—footprints!" Betty Keen called up to him.

The driver looked down at his feet.

Betty Keen looked at the driver with fascination, as though she had not known that the police were like what she saw the driver to be.

"What is it, Roakes?" said Brentford.

Standing on the path, the driver looked down at them. Apparently he found it difficult to say what he had to say in front of Betty Keen and Morris. He considered some way to put it.

Finally, he came out with his pronouncement.

He said, "A person, sir!"

CHAPTER SIX

Brentford followed the driver up the path back to the house. It was not easy, he discovered, to arrive at a coherent story.

He had left Ball to bring the others up from the quay and to keep them off the path. He was not altogether sorry that Betty Keen might have some difficulty in getting back up the bank without the use of the path. Somehow, he had become aware of the intelligence of Betty Keen.

"You say she has lost a daughter?" he said to the driver. They walked between the bushes.

It appeared that that was the substance of the story. Sometimes he was lucky, and evidence came to him, unasked. He never felt very happy when it did. He usually took it to mean that he had exhausted his good luck now, and would have bad luck later.

"So I understand, sir," Roakes said. "Though it wasn't clear. She is distraught."

To Brentford it sounded likely that a woman who had lost a daughter would be distraught. They usually were. He looked back and saw that the others were not following closely.

"Take your time, man, and tell me properly," he said. Before he met the woman, he wanted to know what it was all about.

"I was sitting in the car, sir, listening to the radio. Inspector Crosston was reporting to headquarters that he had found two brassieres and a pair of outsize bloomers."

Brentford wondered if the circumstantial detail was intended to be helpful.

"What happened then?"

"I saw this woman."

"What woman? Where?"

"In the house. That is, she was going to the house. She was in the garden."

"What was she doing when you saw her?"

"Looking at the car, sir."

"Looking at the car?"

"I formed the impression, sir, that she had seen it was a police car."

The car had a large sign on it that said "Police", Brentford remembered. Ahead, lay the house.

He tried to cut the narrative: "So you went and spoke to her?"

"Oh no, sir. You'd told me to keep watch on the radio."

"What did you do?"

"Nothing just then, sir. Inspector Crosston was talking about these bloomers——"

"What did she do?"

"She turned away and went into the house, so I followed her."

"Why?"

The driver turned on the path and looked at Brentford. He said: "It wasn't her house, sir."

It was possible, Brentford realised, that Roakes had placed

the woman as intent on burglary, since he knew the occupants were out. But he did not pursue the matter. To discover the simple facts was difficult enough. When the driver turned to move on again, he stopped him.

"So you followed her into the house?"

"Yes, sir."

"And what did you do?"

"I asked her what she wanted. You see, she looked worried, sir. She said she wanted to speak to Mr. Morris."

"Worried?"

"She had looked worried when she was looking at the police car. She looked more worried when I followed her. I asked her her name, sir, and she said she was Helen Silcrest."

Brentford grunted. Helen Silcrest, he thought. He always had to repeat a name to himself, or he forgot it. But, putting himself in the woman's position, he thought that if he were visiting friends, as he assumed she was, and he found a police car in their drive, and the friends missing, and then was followed into the house by a policeman, he would find it worrying.

Even apart from the question of the missing daughter.

"Where had she come from?"

"I asked her, sir, and she pointed across the lawn and said 'Over there.' Then she sat down in a chair and cried. Then she said she had come to ask if they knew anything about her missing daughter."

From Roakes expression, that was when he had really begun to take an interest.

"This was just now?"

"No, sir. Immediately after you left."

Brentford looked sharply at him.

"I thought to ask her to describe her daughter, sir, to see if it was the right description."

"And?"

"It was, sir, but I had the devil of a job to get it out of her. She said she didn't want to report it to the police just yet. She didn't mean to come to the police yet. That was when she became distraught."

It was possible, Brentford realised. That was when people

31

very often did become distraught, when they realised that they had to make an official matter of whatever was worrying them, and it was not just a temporary and private worry that would be over in a little while.

"All right," Brentford said. He saw that Betty Keen had been got up the bank below them, and the party from the quay were slowly following. He turned to go.

"She said something odd, sir."

Brentford stopped again.

"She said: 'Do you know about her? You know about her! What has she done?'"

Brentford stared at Roakes.

Roakes was edging away from him, looking around the corner of the house at the police car.

"Sir," he said suddenly. "I put her in the car——!"

He had got himself into a position in which he could see the police car. Suddenly, he began to run.

Following at a more even pace, Brentford saw that the car was empty.

Roakes had passed the car and was heading off across the garden, presumably in the direction from which the woman had come. It looked as though he were heading straight for the woods, but if the woman had come that way it had to be assumed there was a path there. Brentford watched Roakes pause, stop, look helpless, stare about him, and start back.

Brentford himself headed for the house. If that was where the woman was going, that, he imagined, would be where she had gone.

CHAPTER SEVEN

"Roakes," said Brentford. "Stop Sergeant Ball and the people who are coming after us, and keep them talking."

The driver had come back to him, and the woman, Helen Silcrest, was visible inside the glass house.

Roakes did not look as though the task he had been given pleased him, nor did he seem too sure he could carry it out, but Brentford ceased to interest himself in him, and turned his attention to the woman.

Inside the house, in the room or subdivided space into which Brentford and Ball had gone, Helen Silcrest was clearly visible, talking into a telephone.

Her actions were normal except that she was talking with what appeared to be undue vehemence and earnestness, and if she had noticed Brentford and Roakes looking at her, she had paid no attention to them. All of which was fairly irrelevant, Brentford imagined, compared to the striking fact that Helen Silcrest was, or rather had once been until fairly recently, one of the most beautiful women he had seen.

She was aged about forty, and inevitably her beauty had begun to deteriorate. It was possible that on that morning the deterioration was more apparent than it would have been had she paid time and attention to her appearance, and not been obsessed with other things. But, looking at her before he went in to her, and before she paid attention to him, Brentford saw in her the full flowering of that quality which he had sensed on sight of the dead girl. Even without the driver's assurance, he would have guessed she was the mother.

Brentford felt pity and self-anger as he went to the door of the house. He knew what he ought to do. He should first question the woman, and discover all he could about the movements of her missing daughter, and then, after that, tell her that her daughter was dead.

The parents of murdered children were very often unable to answer questions very coherently at the time. They tended to regard questions as irrelevant, since they could not bring their child back. Only later, and sometimes too late, they thought in terms of vengeance. Then they wanted to know what the police had done to arrest the killer.

Brentford, walking along the terrace past the window to the door, realised that his actions were bound to be cruel, either way. He watched the woman as he walked. She looked up and saw him as he came into her line of sight. Her eyes widened as though with fear when she saw he was another stranger. She

33

laid down the phone and followed him with her eyes as he reached the door, turned, and came in to her.

Entering the open room, Brentford spoke quietly. "Mrs. Silcrest?"

She looked at him with apprehension and said, "Who are you?"

"Detective Inspector Brentford," Brentford said.

The fear in her eyes became naked. She said, "My God!"

It was not only that he was another stranger instead of her expected friends. It was all too obvious that she connected his rank and title with her missing daughter. Searching as she was, she had every right to be afraid of the sudden appearance of the police in strength. Brentford waited for her to say, "Do you know about my daughter? Where is she?"

Helen Silcrest said: "Have you got Caroline? What has she done?" Her voice was low and exceptionally intense.

Brentford continued to look at her, trying to understand her reaction. The driver had warned him.

The mother, assuming it was the mother, seemed not to think first of something having happened to her daughter, but more of something the daughter might have done. It seemed she would not have been surprised to hear that Caroline, the name she had used, had been arrested.

He tried to make his tone neutral. He said, "Will you describe your daughter, Mrs. Silcrest, and tell me about her movements last night and when you missed her?"

Perhaps a kindliness or pity crept into his tone despite his effort. Helen Silcrest suddenly changed her stance before him and seemed to go out of balance. The tone of her voice rose. She said, "Where is she?"

Colour suddenly flooded her face, to be succeeded by a pallor. She raised a hand towards Brentford as though to fend him off.

"If you could give me a few facts, Madam."

Helen Silcrest suddenly screamed at him: "I have a right to know!"

She had a right, and Brentford could not deny it. But she was distraught already, and he was apprehensive of the effect of telling her. The driver had told him that she was a difficult woman to handle, and he could see she was, as very beautiful women often were.

The situation became more difficult. Out of the corner of his eye, looking past Helen Silcrest, Brentford could see that Roakes and Ball, and Betty Keen and William Morris, had appeared around the corner of the house. Roakes was expostulating, and Morris was arguing with him and trying to push past him in apparent anger. Betty Keen tried to slip past Roakes, who had to move aside to stop her. It would need great tact on Roakes' part, or even on Ball's, to keep the people out of their own house, where they must instantly, on sight of Mrs. Silcrest through the window, realise that a friend was in distress. It was expecting too much.

Brentford realised he had missed his chance or never had one. Helen Silcrest interpreted his glance out of the window and his hesitation as unwillingness. Her expression went beyond fear and became tragic. It was the attitude, it seemed to him, of the commanding beauty who had learned how to make an appeal to get what she wished from life.

"Tell me! You must tell me! You must!" She seemed to sway.

"If we can establish a few facts, Mrs. Silcrest."

"Tell me, do you or don't you have my Caroline?"

It might have been a line from a play, perhaps even a Greek tragedy. But the fact that Helen Silcrest spoke tragic lines did not make her emotion false. The truth was perhaps the other way round, that the tragedians had got the anguish of a beautiful woman right.

Knowing he would have to tell her, Brentford looked with alarm and calculation to the nearest chair. There was perhaps something in his mind. Helen Silcrest was expecting tragedy or something. There was her question about her daughter. But it was clear that when he did tell her, or when she realised from his silence, she was above all not the kind of woman who would quietly and methodically tell him all he had to know.

The inevitable happened. Outside the window, William Morris had looked in, and must have put two and two together. Just as Helen Silcrest was doing, though on a different basis. Helen Silcrest knew her daughter was missing,

35

while William Morris knew there was a body. The sight of Brentford in earnest conversation with Helen Silcrest in his own house seemed to excite him. He might have taken it as an indication that tact was required, that Brentford should be allowed to handle the situation, and that he should stay away, but he did not. William Morris too seemed capable of leaping to conclusions.

"Has something happened to her? Why don't you tell me?"

"Something has happened to someone, Mrs. Silcrest," Brentford said earnestly. "We are trying to find out if it is your daughter. Now if you will tell me——"

William Morris had apparently fired questions at Ball and Roakes about the body or about the situation in the house. He burst through them in a way that would have required more than blocking but physical force to stop him. Brentford had not given orders that he should be kept out at all costs. He came running along the terrace.

"What has happened? Tell me!"

There was no help for it. Brentford had to say, "Mrs. Silcrest, we have found a body."

She swayed, making immediate assumptions, and reached the point of collapse as William Morris came through the door.

"Helen! Surely it can't be Caroline! It can't be!"

William Morris ran forward and helped Brentford to catch the woman. There was something in the way he took hold of her, almost shouldering Brentford aside. It was natural that he should assume that she would prefer to be supported by friends. But he held her intimately, and he gave Brentford a look of near-hate. It was more than a neighbour's action.

He helped her to the chair to which Brentford had been guiding her. "They can't know, Helen! They don't know that the body is Caroline. They don't know whose it is!"

He sounded as though he were telling lies to comfort her. When he had said, "It can't be Caroline," he had not sounded as though he meant it. He sounded very much as though he feared it was Caroline, and had done, ever since he had seen Helen Silcrest talking to Brentford, in a distressed state.

Brentford remembered that Morris had not said where he

36

had been the previous night. Watching his actions, manner and solicitude for Helen Silcrest, Brentford now believed he could guess the reason for that. Betty Keen, entering the house with Ball, seemed to confirm his view. If Morris was more than neighbourly, Betty Keen seemed to keep away from the woman.

Helen Silcrest was sitting looking dazedly and appealingly at William Morris and saying "Caroline?" Her state was as bad, or worse, than Brentford had expected. He turned away to Betty Keen. She seemed to be the one person who was free to be questioned and capable of answering.

"I understand Mrs. Silcrest came looking for her daughter here?" he said.

Betty Keen gave him a strange look. She seemed to disassociate herself from what was going on. If her tone carried any implication, it was that he was addressing his questions to the wrong person.

"Did she?" she said. "I don't know. Why should she?"

She asked Brentford the question that he had been just about to ask her.

But she gave her attention to Brentford. She seemed to regard the sight of Morris and Mrs. Silcrest together not as a neighbour, not even as a stranger, but as though it were something that had nothing to do with her.

"But you know Mrs. Silcrest?" said Brentford sharply.

"Yes. She lives in the next house." Betty Keen nodded in the direction of the lawn.

"Her daughter is called Caroline?"

"Yes."

"How well do you know the daughter?"

"As well as—— As you would expect with the girl next door."

"You can describe her? Will you describe her, please?"

Betty Keen looked from him to the chair occupied by Helen Silcrest. The sight of the mother seemed to remind her.

"Fair haired. Long fair hair. Sixteen in a week or two's time. Normal build. Very pretty."

She was an efficient witness. Brentford said, "Sunburned?"

Betty Keen turned back and glanced sharply at him.

"Yes," she said. "She would be amply sunburned."

Brentford returned her glance. The description was already enough, pending identification of the body, but he thought that Betty Keen might say something of her own accord. She did.

Speaking quietly to him, turned away from the mother and William Morris, she said, "A problem child."

It confirmed a conclusion that Brentford had already come to, but he looked at her questioningly as though he did not understand.

Instead of explaining, Betty Keen said, "They both are."

He realised he would have to question her in detail as soon as he got the chance. He looked at the mother however, who should have been answering the questions.

William Morris had apparently understood something of the situation. He was pleading with Helen Silcrest. "You must pull yourself together, Helen. They need to ask you questions. You must try to help."

If he had stayed out of the house there might have been more chance of that, Brentford thought. With Morris in attendance, Helen Silcrest had relaxed a little, but only to collapse the more.

Brentford looked at the two of them together, and then at the un-neighbourly indifference of Betty Keen, useful as her non-entanglement with the shocked woman was.

He spoke to Morris. "Where is the father?"

Morris looked up as though surprised, as though he had not expected questions to be addressed to him. "He'll be at the house. The house across there."

Brentford turned to Ball, glanced again at the woman, and said, "Send the driver for him, Sergeant." He thought again and stopped Ball as he nodded and began to go out quickly.

"Tell the driver to radio for another car from Crosston," he said. "After the father had been here and I have had a word with him, I may want to send him to view the body."

Ball nodded, expressing his understanding, and went out quickly.

Brentford looked at the room again and thought that, since he had been on the spot when the woman was told, he had got remarkably little information. Then he glanced at Betty Keen, followed Ball out of the house, and stood on the terrace, looking out across the garden.

CHAPTER EIGHT

It had been luck, he thought. At least it had been partly luck that had brought him to the estate. But now, to take the strictly logical view, it was time he went back to Loebeach, set up his headquarters there, and sent out his subordinates to do the leg-work.

Looking at the garden, he thought that there was a kind of mathematical theory of probability about any crime. And in this case the general or ordinary probabilities of crime produced suggestions such as that the murder had been committed by some chance motorist or holidaymaker, who was now fleeing across country and putting as much distance between himself and the scene as possible, or by some villager or boy-friend of the girl's. In either event, if either of these suggestions were the right one, he would work better now from a headquarters at Loebeach.

Betty Keen came out, to stand with him on the terrace overlooking the beautifully arranged garden and the background woods of the Trequayne Estate.

She must have understood his glance, and his intention to question her, he thought. Or perhaps the sight of William Morris, her William Morris, comforting Helen Silcrest, had been too much for her. It was possible that she just did not want to stay in the same room with them.

It was surprising how remote from all that he would be in a headquarters at Loebeach. None of it would emerge from the reports of the detective-sergeants and detective-constables he sent out to do the interviewing in the case.

"What did you mean?" he said to Betty Keen.

While waiting for her answer, he thought that that, perhaps, was the most important usefulness of detectives' reports. They concentrated your mind entirely on what was relevant. They enabled you to see the wood through the trees.

"What did I mean about what?" Betty Keen said, looking intently but passively at the garden.

"You said," he said, " 'They both are.' "

She took a little time to recall the incident. Perhaps she was not in a hurry.

"I was asking you about the girl," he said. "You said she was a problem child. Then you said, 'They both are.' "

"Oh yes," Betty Keen said indifferently. "I was talking about the Silcrest children. They have a son."

"Older or younger than the girl?"

"Aged about ten," she said calmly.

Brentford knew he should be setting up his headquarters now. That was the correct course. Instead, he found himself becoming interested in Betty Keen.

She was paying attention to something other than his questions. He followed the direction of her gaze.

"You are interested in the garden?" he asked.

She gave neither more nor less attention to his irrelevant question than to the relevant ones.

"I spend a lot of time in it, gardening," she said.

It was a sidelight on a woman who, to him, had been merely William Morris's mistress.

Or, Brentford thought, thinking of Morris's attitude with Helen Silcrest, either his ex-mistress, or a mistress cast-off or about to be cast-off. That was the problem. It was possible that all such things were relevant, but it was equally possible that they were highly irrelevant, and had no connection at all with the killing of Caroline Silcrest.

He returned to the main line of his inquiry.

"What was wrong with the children?"

She glanced at him as though wondering why he was asking her that.

"In what way are the problem children problems?" he said with inescapable clarity. He did not think Betty Keen was dull mentally. It seemed more likely that she had become reluctant or deliberately evasive.

"The boy has nervous trouble." Betty Keen looked straight at Brentford. "It is such that they try to keep him away from strangers. You won't be welcome there."

Brentford had not thought he would be welcome, either in the home of the bereaved family or anywhere else. People always thought that the police should question other people.

"And the girl too?" he asked, thinking of Caroline as they had seen her on the beach.

Betty Keen hesitated. "It may have been the same kind of thing," she said. "If you can call it that. To appearances, it looked more as though she was, well, bad."

It was not the impression Brentford had received when he had first seen the pitiful innocence of the body on the beach, but he knew that appearances were deceptive.

"Bad in what way?"

She looked at him resentfully. The girl was dead. "Oh, stealing, a long time ago," she said. She turned away with a shade of anger, as though to go into the house again.

"Miss Keen," he said.

She stopped with the appearances of obedience. Brentford had just decided what appearances were.

"I still have to ask you where Mr. Morris was last night," he said.

She made a small gesture. It was as though she dismissed that problem, thought nothing of it. The one thing she did not appear to be was disturbed.

She looked at the garden again.

"You can ask him."

"I am asking you."

"He was here most of the time. I did not follow him when he went out."

"Miss Keen, we found the body not far from here. It is up to you to help us."

She turned her calm gaze on to him. He was surprised at its calmness. Most people would have been disturbed at his implication, whether innocent or guilty.

"William is not that kind of man," she said.

She spoke quite clearly, as someone who knew, in her own mind, what kinds of men there were.

"Do you mind answering questions?" Brentford asked her abruptly.

"What do you want to know?" she asked shortly.

"More about the character of the dead girl for a start."

Brentford tried to understand the play of her expression. She did not answer.

"Have you any idea why she was only missed this morning?" he said. "She must have been gone last night."

She did not say she could not answer. That was what was remarkable, her mingling of reticence and honesty.

"You should ask the parents that, Inspector. I have no intention of answering for them."

Yet what she had already said had been enough for Brentford to build up a hypothesis, if not a theory.

"'Bad,'" he quoted. "You said she was a problem child. But I understood you to mean that she was bad now, or until now. Not long ago in the past."

She stared at him.

Somewhat sharply, he said, "What kind of badness? Boys?"

He felt she must see the relevance of that, and how important it was that he should have an answer.

"Or men?" he asked. "At her age, she had a man friend?"

She coloured slightly. She did not answer. Her failure to answer caused Brentford to build up the question in a way he would not otherwise have done. After all, he could have been mistaken about the signs he had seen.

"Mr. Morris?" he said.

At that she laughed, with a slightly high note.

"Inspector, for heaven's sake!"

Brentford looked at her soberly and seriously. "You see to what a failure to answer questions may lead," he said.

She turned, moved her foot on the ground, looked down at it, and appeared chastened.

"You saw William with the mother, Helen Silcrest, Inspector," she said quietly. "I know he is reluctant to say where he was last night, but you can guess, surely. He was only out a short time. I think you, as well as I, could put two and two together without making any suggestions about poor Caroline."

When she spoke in that way, Betty Keen gave every indication of sincerity. What was remarkable was the way she combined it with an almost serene reference to a possible liaison between her lover and another woman.

Yet she contrived to make it clear that she did not think she was the right person to ask about the Silcrests, not even about the essential details of their family life. She spoke as though she was aware she had a prejudice and that anything she might say might be misleading.

She was relieved of the need to say more as it happened, for Brentford was watching the drive, and he saw two cars arriving. One of them was his own car, which would be bringing the father of the dead girl, and the other would be the spare car from Crosston, which he intended to use to send the father to see the body.

"All right, Miss Keen," he said abruptly, and walked away towards the front of the house.

He did not tell her that she and William Morris might be questioned again later, but perhaps that was hardly necessary.

CHAPTER NINE

The cars had stopped when he reached the drive. The man getting out of his own car was ordinary-looking, of mediocre appearance, and going bald. Brentford looked at him and thought how remarkable it was that such a man should have a wife like Helen Silcrest and should have had a daughter like the girl on the beach.

"Inspector Brentford? You asked for a car, sir?" The driver of the spare car stopped him in passing.

Brentford nodded. "Stand by." He went on to meet Ball and his own car's passenger. Ball, after consulting the driver, came forward to introduce them.

"This is Mr. George Silcrest, Inspector. Mr. Silcrest, this is Inspector Brentford, in charge of the case."

They met in the open, and Brentford was consciously platitudinous when he said, "This is a bad business, Mr. Silcrest."

There was too little he could say to the man with the shrinking, anxious look. It was better, he had discovered long ago, to say the simple, obvious things that a man in such a situation would recognise, and at least, though worried and pale, Silcrest did not look on the point of collapse.

"My wife——?" Silcrest said, and looked towards the house.

Painful as it was, Brentford felt he should question the man before he reached his wife, even though it meant doing it in the open. Once with his wife, it was very likely that George Silcrest would have his mind on other things than answering questions, and it was a defect of the Morris house as a scene for operations that it did not have separate rooms.

"She is in the house being taken care of, Mr. Silcrest. I have to ask you——"

"Who is with her?"

Brentford wished he knew whether the particular anxious look Silcrest cast towards the house was his normal attitude or something arising out of the immediate circumstances. It was a by no means unfamiliar difficulty. When people were met in circumstances of sudden death and bereavement, it was often almost impossible to guess what they were like in their normal lives. Under normal conditions, when not being held by a policeman in the driveway of a house and questioned about a missing daughter, their whole manner, outlook and attitude might be altogether different.

"Mr. Morris is with her, sir," Brentford said, and watched Silcrest to see if he showed any particular reaction to that information, significant as he felt it might be.

There was no obvious anger or increased distress. It was possible that Silcrest did not care who was with his wife, so long as someone was, in the light of more important events. Yet he had asked the question, and he made as though to go to the house.

"I'm afraid before you go I have to ask you when you last saw your daughter," Brentford said.

Silcrest stared and said, "Your man said something about having to see a body."

"Let's do it this way, Mr. Silcrest," Brentford said gently.

"First, I want to ask you one or two questions, as short as possible. Then you can see your wife. Then the car will take you."

Silcrest looked as though so much formality in the proceedings frightened him, realising that matters were not under his control.

"Just when did you miss your daughter, sir?" Brentford said insistently.

"Hasn't Helen told you?"

"No." Brentford felt it best not to elaborate on Helen Silcrest's state of shock.

Silcrest looked at him dazedly and said, "We were out. When we came home, we assumed she had gone to bed, so you see we didn't see her."

"You were both out, you and Mrs. Silcrest?"

"Yes. Helen was back when I came home. She didn't say anything."

Brentford tried not to ask unnecessary questions. From Silcrest's answer, he gathered that Mr. and Mrs. Silcrest had gone out separately, not together.

"What time did you get back, sir?"

"About midnight. I don't know exactly."

"So you actually last saw your daughter much earlier than that. When would that be?"

Silcrest looked as though he tried to think and said, "At dinner."

"Was she intending to stay in or go out, sir?"

Silcrest hesitated, but then spoke definitely. "We told her to stay in. We have a son, Clarence, who requires constant supervision. I didn't think she'd be so disobedient as to leave him and go out, but it seems she did."

Brentford remembered what Betty Keen had told him, that they were "both problem children".

"You say your son requires constant supervision? I understood from the neighbours that he is aged ten, sir."

"Clarence has a nervous disorder. There are behaviour problems."

"Your son isn't big for his age, or—awkward?" Brentford said.

45

Silcrest looked at Brentford as though he were slightly mad. "Clarence is a weak, sick boy. Good heavens, Inspector, you can't suggest——!"

"No, sir," Brentford said hastily. In view of the ages of the children, it was unlikely that the boy would have had anything to do with the crime anyway. "So you last saw your daughter at dinner. How was she dressed?"

He was glad to get back to the essential, routine questions, and he noticed that Silcrest had less hesitation than most fathers in remembering what his daughter had been wearing when he had last seen her the day before.

"I believe she was wearing her blue dress. Yes. And white shoes and socks."

Despite the unconventional scene for the questions, in the driveway, Silcrest had yielded much solid information, and the last item might be invaluable to Crosston's men who were searching for the clothes.

"But she may have changed, of course," Brentford said.

Silcrest did not deny it. Instead, he began to say, with increasing horror, "Your man said you had found a body——!"

"Try to think, Mr. Silcrest," Brentford said. "Just when and how did you actually miss your daughter. And supposing she went out after you had told her not to, have you any idea where she would have gone?"

He succeeded in staving off Silcrest's crisis for a little longer. With his attention caught by the questions, Silcrest stared back at him with a strange expression and said, "I can't believe . . . !" Then he answered the factual question almost in passing. "At breakfast time this morning. Helen called her, but she did not come down. She went up to look, since she didn't answer, and she wasn't there."

Brentford had noticed the hesitation and change of subject. For the moment, he asked, "Had the bed been slept in?"

"No." Silcrest was as definite as he could be under the trying circumstances. "Helen said not. She said, 'She hasn't been to bed'."

Brentford frowned at the man. It was true he was questioning him in an awkward time and place, but it did not seem to him that Silcrest was telling him all he knew or could guess about his daughter's disappearance.

"I want you to think of this, Mr. Silcrest."

Silcrest did not look as though he wanted to think of anything. He looked at the house as though he wanted to go to his wife.

"You knew at breakfast time this morning that your daughter had disappeared some time the previous night, didn't you, Mr. Silcrest?" Brentford said. "Yet the police received no call from you. We only heard about your daughter when your wife happened to come here, and even then she did not approach us at once, or even seem to be looking for your daughter, but rather her intention seemed to be to talk to Mr. Morris. Isn't it possible therefore that, when you found your daughter missing, you thought of at least somewhere where she might be?"

Silcrest stared back at Brentford as though he did not know whether to speak or not.

"If you will think, I think you will decide you want to help us all you can," said Brentford.

"We thought—I thought—she must have gone to David Feltham's," Silcrest blurted out.

"David Feltham's?" Brentford said. He seemed to have heard the name. He remembered. By the creek, Morris had given him the names of the people on the estate.

"The house over there," Silcrest said, and pointed. It was not in the direction of his own house, but at right angles to it, away from the creek and across the estate towards the sea.

The explanation seemed to Brentford to involve more problems than it solved.

"Didn't you at once try to confirm that?" he asked. He looked around at the estate. "Presumably you are all on the phone?"

He remembered Helen Silcrest phoning from the Morris house, however.

Silcrest's expression had changed. He was suddenly showing more distress. He said, "Inspector, do you have to ask me these questions here and now?" It was only after he had made his protest that he said, in a low voice, "David Feltham and I are not on speaking terms. That is why I didn't phone him. I told Helen she shouldn't. I don't know whether she did or not."

The protest was legitimate. It was not a matter that the man could be expected to go into while standing in the drive, waiting to join his distressed wife and then to go to view what was almost certainly his daughter's body.

"All right, Mr. Silcrest," Brentford said heavily, and moved aside as an indication that the father could go on to the house.

He made the mental reservation that it never would seem to be the time to go into the situation, whatever it was, about which Silcrest was hinting. Just before or after he viewed the body would be a time when it would be even more difficult for Silcrest to talk about it. Yet the fact that the father suspected that the daughter was with a man with whom he was not on speaking terms was a thing that would have to be investigated very thoroughly. It was only, Brentford thought, that there were other ways of doing it than through the father.

Silcrest moved to go, then turned back on Brentford.

"Who is to look after Clarence while I am doing all this?" he said.

"Perhaps your wife will be in a condition to go home now," Brentford suggested. "Or perhaps there is some other woman on the estate who will take her home and stay with her?"

"Who?" said Silcrest in a voice that rose. "Who are you suggesting? Mrs. Morris, or Mrs. Trueman-Davies?"

The thing that was odd to Brentford's ears was that he seemed to be suggesting that while Betty Keen was unsuitable as a comforter of his wife and guardian of his child, the other woman on the estate, a Mrs. Trueman-Davies, was hardly less so.

But at least he did not seem to expect Brentford to answer his questions. He went away along the terrace towards the entrance to the house as though the problem would solve itself.

Which it did, Brentford noticed. While he was briefing the driver of the spare car and considering whether he had not better regard himself as temporarily finished with the Morris house and prepare to move elsewhere, the people came out of the house again.

It was William Morris who was taking Helen Silcrest home, in Morris's own car; and her husband, after what could not have been at all a long talk with her, came back to be sent to view the body with an attitude that was at once permissive, and outraged and indignant. It was as though he found himself in a position in which he had to give another man's relations with his wife an almost official sanction.

CHAPTER TEN

That was it, Brentford thought ten minutes later. Thick. He was looking out through the windscreen of the car at the tangled woodland of the Trequayne Estate. But it was not the tangled woodland around the stationary car at the junction of the drives that he thought was thick. It was the human relations and mutual involvement of all the people on the estate, the relatives and neighbours surrounding the dead girl.

He had ordered Roakes to stop the car after they had driven away from Morris's house, and now he and Ball and the driver sat looking at nothing but the summery undergrowth and trees while he decided at a little length upon his next move.

The fact that the relationships of the people, the adults around the dead girl, were tangled, was not in any way a proof that they were relevant. His situation in the car in the quiet woodland was very apt, he thought. So long as he was in it, he could not see the wood for the trees. To see the woodland and the estate as a whole, he would have to get out of it, and view it from the outside.

The driver moved. "Would you like a cup of coffee, sir?" Roakes asked, searching in the capacious pockets of the car. Not knowing the reason for the delay, Roakes thought the time suitable to prove his usefulness as a driver by producing a flask of hot coffee.

Ball, sitting in the back seat with Brentford, looked at the Inspector with more reservation. "Yes, if you have any coffee, Roakes, we might have it now," he said. Ball knew that Brentford had reached a point where he had to make an either-or decision.

The fact that the car had been stopped showed that Brentford was not finding it easy.

"None of all this is getting us any nearer the holidaymaker or beatnik vagabond who might have done it," Ball observed dryly.

Ball had a capacity for saying things that could be taken one way or the other. He was certainly not saying that some unknown stranger had committed the murder. He was just holding the idea up for inspection.

Brentford inspected it, or rather continued to do so. He had already had it in mind that if he were to see the crime in terms as broad as that, as an event about which nothing had yet been proved, then the way to do it was to return to a head-quarters, examine the lists, which the police were so fond of making, of strangers in the area, and start the methodical, routine check on the movements of everyone within an area of, say, five miles of the creek.

But it was not possible both to do that and to go into more intimate and closer detail about the lives of the people in the Trequayne Estate. The kind of nuances and relationships he had been observing simply did not emerge from official police reports.

If Brentford had sent a team of detectives into the estate to do what he had done himself that morning, the only thing that would have emerged ultimately from their reports would have been that Betty Keen was not Mrs. Morris.

He was still thinking of the problem when the police loud-speaker in the car, which had been muttering away occasion-ally with routine messages, burst into life with something more relevant. "Peter King Thirteen," it said in a female voice.

Roakes turned in his seat, looked at Brentford, and said, "That's us."

"Answer, but don't say I'm here," said Brentford cautiously.

The driver picked up his phone and made the call. They watched him while the girl said, "I have a message for Inspector Brentford." Roakes glanced at Brentford and said, "I will deliver it."

"Superintendent Crawford to Inspector Brentford," the girl said. "Urgent report local headquarters for Loebeach crime. Lacking information. Crawford."

While the driver acknowledged receipt, Brentford and Ball looked at one another. It seemed that Brentford's doubts were being resolved by his superior.

It was more than a direct hint that the Superintendent expected the local headquarters to be set up and the routine inquiries to be carried out.

"He has some information now," Brentford said. "He has someone on their way to identify the body."

Brentford was not the kind of man to react tamely to pressure. He had been in doubt before, but now he was in less doubt.

Ball wisely said nothing.

"Give them this reply," Brentford said to Roakes. "Local inquiries yielding results. Continuing in view of possibility of early arrest."

"Are you expecting an early arrest, sir?" Ball said.

"No," said Brentford, and watched Roakes pass the message.

Ball looked a little unhappy. For Brentford to go against the wishes of the Superintendent would be acceptable only if positive results were achieved, it seemed to him.

"Well?" Brentford said, watching his expression.

"If it's this business of a Mr. David Feltham, I could interview him," Ball said.

"Certainly you could, Sergeant," Brentford said. "And no one better. But could you tell me the exact meaning of everything he said afterwards?"

Ball looked doubtful. He was not entirely sure that he knew what Brentford meant, far less the possible meaning of a hypothetical statement from a Mr. David Feltham.

"It will probably only take five minutes," Brentford said with more optimism than was justified by events on the estate so far. "Either he will clear himself quite easily, or I shall have to interview him myself later. It will save time if I do it in the first place while I am already on the spot."

Ball did not actually mind if Brentford did all the work himself. It certainly saved him a great deal of trouble caused by taking down statements, typing them out, and then putting them in the waste-paper basket.

Roakes looked at Brentford, watched his nod, and started the engine.

"Where to, sir?" he said. "Do we know where this Mr. Feltham's house is?"

"Towards the sea," Brentford said, looking through the impenetrable woods of the estate. "Go back to the main drive, and continue right through, and maybe we'll come to it."

He was hopefully oblivious of the fact that it would probably take them more than five minutes to find David Feltham, far more to interview him and finish with him.

CHAPTER ELEVEN

The peninsula was triangular, they discovered, and Feltham's house was situated on the farther side, which was farthest from the creek.

It was not that they had difficulty finding it. They had only to continue beyond the branching drives to the Morris's and the Silcrests' to come to it. The remaining drive led in the wrong direction, and was presumably the Trueman-Davies's. What surprised them was that they came to a house at all, and not simply to the sea.

The woods gave way to bracken and open ground with briars, and they stopped the car at the end of the drive when they saw the house before them, with a blue summer sky behind it that had the shade and intensity of light sky over seaward cliffs.

It was brighter and warmer in the sunlight out of the woods, and they had a considerable area of garden to cover before they reached the gay-looking house with its venetian blinds and sunshades. The house was as modern as Morris's, though of a different design, and Brentford and Ball approached it through the garden with methodical anticipation, as though they were stalking a major quarry.

In fact their attitude would have been just the same if they had been going to ask Mr. Feltham if he had a licence for his dog. They stopped in the garden and looked at the plants, and Ball said, "If he lives alone, he doesn't do all this himself."

They had not heard of a Mrs. David Feltham.

Brentford read the signs with an Englishman's appreciation of the psychological significance of someone else's garden.

"Landscaped by a specialist firm," he judged. "He could keep it in order with a jobbing gardener." He looked at the path that ran to the house, and at a branch that ran round it, to the sea.

A man appeared at the door as though he had seen them through the window and was impatient of their delay.

He was a thin, slightly undersized, distinguished-looking man, immaculately dressed in white shirt and grey trousers. The meticulousness of his appearance was enhanced by the fact that he looked extremely clean.

They did not hurry, and he came down the path to meet them.

"Who are you? Why are you here?" he said with a shade of sharpness.

But he did not look at them as though he was wondering who they were. He looked at them as though he knew what they were and as though he was wondering what to do with them.

It was possible that his sharpness was induced by nerves. His manner seemed nervous. It would not have needed a great deal of exaggeration to say that at first sight it seemed guilty.

Brentford stood in the warm, sunlit and very pleasant garden, and said, "Mr. Feltham?"

Receiving only a look from the man, he spoke formally.

"I am Chief Detective Inspector Brentford, and this is Detective Sergeant Ball."

He was not quite sure why he gave their titles in full. It was

53

more usual to shorten them or to play them down a little, not to alarm a stranger. But since he had given them in full, it was a little unfair to notice how, on hearing them, Feltham seemed to be taken aback and to freeze.

"We would like a word with you, sir," Brentford said.

Feltham's thin, rather fine face worked in a nervous way. It was a little like the motions of the face of a man with an habitual stutter. Yet they had not noticed that Feltham had any tendency to stutter.

"You are Mr. Feltham, aren't you, sir?" Brentford said.

"Yes!" Feltham seemed to come to the surface with difficulty. He turned on the path, not towards the house but half away from them. "'Mr.' not 'Dr.' I am—before I retired—I am a surgeon."

It was only reasonable that, Brentford having given his credentials, Feltham should give his. But it did not get them any farther.

"Shall we step up to the house, sir?" Brentford said.

Feltham turned back and faced them.

"What do you want to speak to me about?"

Brentford put Feltham down as an intelligent man.

"There has been some trouble on the estate this morning, sir."

"Yes—and you want to see me?"

"Do you think we should talk inside?" Brentford said, wondering if he was going to dispose of Feltham as quickly as he hoped, after certain not very conclusive signs.

"Yes!" said Feltham. "Forgive me." Turning to lead them up to the house, he spoke to them with apology.

"I have a man who comes from the village to attend to the garden, but no one in the house."

"I shouldn't worry if you're not ready to receive us, sir."

"It isn't that!"

Ball put in a pacifying word. "The garden must take a lot of your time all the same, sir," he said. There was something about Ball, about the satisfying way he said things, which sometimes helped to put things in proportion for a nervous witness.

Feltham turned on his heel and looked at him. They had a

54

picture of a different Feltham, with much self-certainty and an acid tongue. "Can you suggest any better way of spending time?" he said. Then Feltham paused. He seemed scared by what he had done in his reprimand of Ball. He gave Brentford a strange look. "Yes, I must speak to you," he said to Brentford.

"You must speak to us, sir?" Brentford said in a neutral tone.

He noticed that they were making their way to the house in abortive and uneasy stages, as though Feltham did not want to take them there.

"About Caroline," said Feltham.

Brentford stopped: "What about Caroline?"

"She has been murdered?" Feltham said.

"Who told you she had been murdered, sir?"

Feltham went on into the house. He did not wait for Brentford, who had to follow him though he would rather have stayed where they were outside and continued the conversation at just that point.

Brentford rarely forgot just how much, or usually how little, he had told anyone he was interviewing. When they knew more than he had told them, he wanted to know how. But as he expected, their belated and slightly difficult entry of the house overlaid that for the moment.

"I'll take you to the living-room," Feltham said, standing waiting for them in the hall.

He said it as though he had come to a positive decision about it, though, due to the construction of the house, it was hard to see where else he could have taken them.

The hall extended, with long windows and indoor plants like the Morrises, all down one side of the house. With windows down one side and a garden door at each end, the exits from it were by way of two doors and a stairway on the other side. One of the doors was open and revealed a kitchen such as only a bachelor who took a fastidious delight and pride in his preparation of food would have. The other door, when Feltham opened it, led to a large living-room which covered all the rest of the ground floor.

The room was full of flowers.

Ball frowned, and Brentford looked at them with curiosity as Feltham ushered them in. They were not growing flowers or indoor plants of the kind in which the well-provided people of the Trequayne estate seemed to specialise. They were garden flowers, recently cut and fresh, and they were arranged in vases, and distributed in such ample variety in all available places that the room looked as though it had been decorated for a wedding.

Feltham, having allowed them to precede him into the room, stood in the doorway looking at it as though he were only just seeing it as it would appear to them, and although he had made the decision, he was regretting now, desperately and too late, that he had ever let them into it.

"Who told you that Caroline Silcrest had been murdered, sir?" Brentford asked him.

Feltham stared at him and at his room. Then he came in. He looked about him as though the flowers had a significance for him. Then he looked again at Brentford. He did not seem to draw any comfort from the sight. On the contrary, the presence of Brentford seemed to confirm some fact or supposition he had been thinking. He did not ask them to sit down, but he went into the centre of the room himself and found a chair. He sat down and put his head in his hands. It was not, so far as they could judge, the kind of action that could possibly be normal to Feltham.

"Obviously you will suspect me," he said, speaking clearly but with his head down and not looking up at them.

Brentford and Ball exchanged a glance, and Ball took out his notebook.

"Why should we suspect you, sir?" Brentford said in the deliberate, neutral tone he had adopted.

"For God's sake!" Feltham said, suddenly looking up at them with a face that was strained and anxious to the point of desperation. "Don't you know? Has no one told you? I—I must——— In all decency, Inspector, can't you give me five minutes before you ask me to make a statement———?"

He looked at them pleadingly, and as though there was no thought in his mind but that they had come to him specifically to accuse him of the murder.

56

CHAPTER TWELVE

They walked down the path again, not hastily, not going anywhere, but giving Feltham what he had asked, five minutes, which Brentford was checking by his watch.

Ball was nervous about it. He could not see why Brentford should do it. He looked back quickly at the house from time to time, as though he half expected Feltham to be caught running off for the woods, or at least emerging from the back door.

Brentford rather took the edge off his apparent kindness to Feltham.

"This is for us rather than for him," he said. "If there is something so obvious that it points to him as the murderer, the question is why we weren't told of it by anyone except by him."

Walking reluctantly down the garden path, Ball mentally reviewed cases in which people had confessed to things they had not done.

"Perhaps they did not know that whatever it is points to him," he said. "Except the father."

"He seems to think they would. And with the Morrises and the parents, we have seen the majority of the people on the estate. There are only some people called Trueman-Davies we have not seen."

"Or maybe they did tell us. Why did we come to see him? Didn't the parents tell you there was something between them and him about the girl?"

"How many fathers have you met, who have lost a teen-age daughter, murdered?"

"Three I suppose. It depends what you mean by met. You could maybe stretch it to half a dozen."

"Have you met one of them who, in the moment he learned about the crime, didn't name a name, if he could possibly think of one, and say outright 'He is the one who did it'?"

"Death takes people different ways. Look how shocked

Morris was. It didn't produce that reaction in his woman—Betty Keen."

"She's another. I had quite a talk with her. She had every chance to tell me."

"What are you going to do now?" Ball said, looking at the car which stood at the end of the drive before them. "This is going to take some time. You can see that. Will you send another message to the Super saying you're expecting another arrest at any moment?"

He turned round and looked back at the house.

"He's probably committing suicide now," he said. "I've never known anyone leave a suspect alone before."

Brentford too looked at the car and then back at the house.

"What I want to know and need to know," he said, "is the doctor's more detailed report about the body." Then, looking at the house, he said quietly:

"If he is guilty, do you want to stop him committing suicide?"

Ball looked shocked. He had never heard of such a wilful departure from police procedure as Brentford seemed to be suggesting.

But he was a practical man. "How would you explain it if he did?" he said.

"The truth. He asked us to wait while he considered matters before he made a statement. He has a right to do that. When we came back we found him dead."

"You'd get a rocket. Failure in your duty to bring him up for trial."

"That's how they reward you for saving ten thousand pounds of the taxpayers' money."

Ball looked at Brentford uncertainly. He did not know if he were serious or not.

"It would need a different legal system," he said, "to give the accused a chance to commit suicide before he came up for trial."

"I know," Brentford said. "I invented it." He turned slowly and began to walk back up towards the house.

"Do you want anything, sir?" the driver said, seeing them turn back before they reached the car.

Brentford looked back and shook his head.

"Not now, Roakes. If anyone wants to know where I am, I'm interviewing a man who wants to make a statement."

Both Ball and the driver looked dubiously at Brentford, doubting if it was enough to keep a whole police force quiet.

But Brentford went up the hill to the house, and it was probably true that they would not interrupt him while he was actually in process of taking the statement.

"I don't think I quite understood, sir," Ball said, "what you said this morning about treating the case as though the girl were still alive."

Brentford shook his head.

"Murdered bodies live," he said. "You think about it. They cause more stir and have more effect on people than they could if they were still alive."

It was too metaphysical for Ball. Or perhaps he did not think that metaphysics mixed with police work.

"He's still alive," he said, indicating the house. "I saw him at the window."

It was true. They could see Feltham appearing and re-appearing at the window as though he were pacing up and down his room.

"A pity," Brentford said with compassion.

Ball looked shocked again.

"You don't know what questions to ask about a statement," Brentford said, "until you hear it." He was thinking of himself, of the mental strain.

The sunlight was becoming hotter. Ball sympathised with Brentford, and ran his finger round his own collar. It was a beautiful summer's day, and he could think of better things to do than taking a statement from a possible murderer.

"I suppose you will want it recorded?" he said.

"Every word," said Brentford. "And now he's had a chance to think about it, it should be really good."

Ball himself no longer looked so pleased about the prospect.

"And long," Brentford said. "You know what statements are like, from people who are educated, intelligent and articulate."

"He's a surgeon," Ball said. "Compared with other doctors, they are sometimes short and crisp."

59

Brentford seemed struck by that, and paused as they reached the door.

"Doesn't he strike you as rather young to be retired, for a surgeon?"

Ball grunted. Brentford was not ahead of him.

"They all are," he said. "He's the third, and not one of them yet is at the normal age you'd expect of people who are retired."

Brentford was thoughtful as they went back to the flower-filled room. The flowers had a heavy scent.

CHAPTER THIRTEEN

Feltham had sat down again, in the same chair as before, with a large vase of flowers on the table beside him, but this time, when they went in, they too sat down.

They chose positions from which they could get the light on Feltham's face. He looked pale but composed, with the damp, slightly parted lips of a man about to walk a tight-rope.

"If you're going to make a statement, sir," Brentford said comfortably, "we'd better begin with some details such as your full name and age and a little about your former history."

Ball carefully did not meet his eye. There was no need to alert Feltham about what they did not know, but needed to know, about the Trequayne estate.

Feltham frowned. He looked like a man who had so much to say that he found the preliminaries distracting and a waste of time.

"I told you. My name is David Feltham. I was a surgeon. A consultant surgeon. The only point that need concern you is that I was a consultant gynaecologist at the Mary Cross Nursing Home in London West Ten."

Brentford glanced at Ball. He did not know how the information Feltham gave could concern them, but he wanted to see that Ball got it down.

"Age?" he said.

"Fifty-two."

It was older than Feltham looked.

"Have you been retired long, sir?"

"Five years. I came here when these houses were built, as everyone else did."

That made Feltham only forty-seven, Brentford noticed, when, as a consultant surgeon, he had retired. Ball looked as though he were doing written arithmetic in his notebook.

"Right, sir. Now shall we move on to your connection with the girl you call Caroline?"

Feltham looked uneasy.

"I retired for personal reasons," he said.

"Yes, sir," said Brentford.

"I had made enough money; this estate was being built; I saw it and liked it and chose to retire," said Feltham.

"Yes, Mr. Feltham," said Brentford.

"Aren't you going to ask me how I knew that Caroline had been murdered before you came here?" Feltham said.

Brentford looked at him gravely. "I was going to ask that," he said. "In due course, Mr. Feltham, we would have come to that."

"I'll tell you now," Feltham said.

"It's as you wish, Mr. Feltham. Since you have volunteered a statement, you can, naturally, say anything you wish."

Feltham looked a little bitter. "Aren't you going to warn me that anything I say will be taken down and may be used in evidence against me?"

"Any statement may be used in evidence, Mr. Feltham. That is what it is for."

"But you don't caution me?"

"I haven't arrested you or warned you of an impending prosecution yet, Mr. Feltham. Do you think there is some reason why I should do that?"

"I think you may think it when you hear what I have to say," said Feltham.

"Suppose you just say what you have to say, Mr. Feltham," Brentford said earnestly, "and let me be the judge of that."

Feltham looked as though he wished there was some other way of doing it.

"We haven't got very far yet, Mr. Feltham," Brentford said.

"All right. I had two phone calls this morning. I mean three calls, but from two people."

"You would like to tell us about these?"

"Yes. The first was early. About—Oh, about two hours ago or a little more. It was from Mrs. Silcrest. She was disturbed. She said: 'Is Caroline with you?' And when I said she wasn't, she said: 'You must send her home'."

"And what was your reaction to that?"

"I was worried."

"Why?"

"It wasn't sensible. You understand? She asked if she was here, and it was when I said she wasn't that she said 'You must send her home'. She sounded vague and stupid."

"Was that the only reason you were worried?"

Feltham looked worried at the telling of it.

"Wouldn't you like to hear of the other two calls before we go into that?"

"As you wish, Mr. Feltham."

"She called again later. Mrs. Silcrest. About an hour ago. She sounded more disturbed. Very disturbed and even less sensible. I can't tell you all she said. She began by saying I must send Caroline home. I said she wasn't here again. She said she must be. They knew she was. By 'they' I assumed she meant herself and her husband. I said Caroline wasn't here. I was—forceful about it. She said they hadn't seen her since last night, and that her bed had not been slept in. I said she must look elsewhere. I must admit that what she said disturbed me. She said she was looking elsewhere. She was phoning from the Morrises. She began to say something about the police. I don't know what she was saying about the police. Somehow I gathered she was threatening me with something. Then her conversation broke off. She said something about 'someone here'. But when I asked her what, she had put the receiver down."

Brentford looked at Feltham silently. He saw no point in

telling Feltham that he was the 'someone', in all probability, who had interrupted that call made by Mrs. Silcrest from the Morris house.

"You say you were disturbed?"

"Naturally. I wondered what had happened to the girl."

"Just that? You had been told the girl was missing and you wondered what had happened to her?"

"I didn't say that."

"You mean you were especially worried?"

Feltham paused and looked grey. When he began again, it was in a lower voice.

"I had another call," he said. He seemed to choose deliberately that way to tell it. "I told you I had three, and this was from the other person. From Betty Morris. It was—only a few minutes before you came. She spoke urgently. 'Do you know anything about Caroline, about Caroline Silcrest?' she said. 'It's important, David.' I told her about the two calls I had had from Helen. I thought that was the best way to tell her what I knew. She said, 'Yes, but do you know anything about her, where she was last night?' I felt alarmed. I said: 'What is it, Betty?' and she said: 'They've found a body!' I don't know what I said to that. I think it was something stupid. I think I asked her where. I must have, because she said: 'In the creek!' I said: 'Good God! Do you think it might be her?' She said: 'The police were here and they seemed to think so. They wouldn't, would they, if it were someone else or a different kind of body?' I said: 'Good God! She drowned herself!' And she said: 'What are you saying, David?' I said: 'How could she drown herself in the creek, when she could swim quite well?' She said: 'David, you don't understand. The inspector who was here distinctly said that she had been murdered.' But I don't know what I said to that."

Feltham looked up at Brentford.

"You see it was a shock to me," he said. "It still is. I can't get over it. You see, Caroline was here until a late hour last night. I mean here, in this room. And it looks awkward for me, Inspector. So much so that when you first appeared I didn't know whether to reserve my defence, to lie to you, or tell you the truth or what. That's why I asked you to leave me alone for a moment. I was in such an awkward position that I did not know what to do about it. I mean, a girl of her age and a man of mine. I simply had to think."

Feltham looked Brentford directly in the eye.

He said: "I'm telling the truth, Inspector."

He looked more unduly disturbed than anything he had said would explain.

CHAPTER FOURTEEN

It was quiet in the room.

A bee was buzzing against the glass of a window covered with a venetian blind, and another was moving slumberously about the room, lazily, as though it did not know the flowers were cut and believed it had found a garden. It moved from flower to flower, and one window pane was open, allowing the bees and air to enter, while outside the light on the lawn was strengthening as time passed and the day approached the full heat of midday.

Brentford continued to look at Feltham for a moment, then glanced at Ball, who nodded. He had got it all down so far. Feltham's narrative might be involved, and he was too obviously a man who preferred the oblique approach and seemed to shrink from the simple presentation of naked facts, but it was at least coherent.

Some people could not tell a story at all, and ventured far into irrelevancies, but they did not get that feeling about Feltham. Every word he said had meaning, sometimes too much. As to whether a mind that could handle a long and complex narrative in that way was to be trusted, that was another matter.

Brentford had to remind himself that because a man was intelligent, that did not necessarily imply that he was guilty.

"Mr. Feltham," he said, "since you are making a voluntary statement I have no need to caution you. I will do something for you, however, beyond my line of duty. Do you want to see a lawyer?"

Feltham thought about it, sitting leaning forward slightly in his chair and looking at the floor.

He looked up. "You are in charge of this case?" he asked.

"Yes," Brentford said. "For the moment I am. But I can't promise you anything, Mr. Feltham. I am naturally at the mercy of my superiors, and in a case like this there is always the chance that the Superintendent himself may take over, or he may call in Scotland Yard. It depends on his view of the progress I am making."

The Superintendent, Brentford thought, would by now be in touch with Crosston. They would have discussed Brentford's irregular actions and, with the best will in the world, Crosston would only be able to tell him that Brentford had left him in charge of the scene of the crime and the inevitable and extending search for the clothes. Apart from that, Brentford had disappeared into the estate. The production of someone to identify the body, and a message to the effect that the search should be extended across the creek, might not be taken as adequate for the man who was presumed to keep his head clear, take charge perhaps of a dragnet across the county, and who had made no reports at all.

An act of faith, Brentford realised. That was what he was involuntarily demanding of his colleagues. And someone would have to be dealing with other matters, such as reports of suspicious characters seen around the countryside, which should rightfully be his. No, therefore. He could not promise Feltham that the exact circumstances in which a man made a voluntary statement that might incriminate himself would be fully taken into account by whoever was in charge of the case in its later stages. He had not that much faith in himself.

"I will tell you everything I know, none-the-less," said Feltham. "No, I don't want to defer my statement until I have seen a lawyer. I am thrusting myself on your mercy to some extent, am I not?"

Brentford looked at him gravely. He wished he could say something like, "A man who tells the police the whole truth, right out and to begin with, never has cause to regret it later."

65

But he could not. If Feltham ever were accused of the crime, it would not be Brentford, but a trained lawyer or prosecuting counsel, who would look at his original statement, without mercy and with the definite intention of making a case out of it, as would be his brief. It was not the business of such people to decide on guilt. A court would do that. All they would have to discover was whether they could make a case.

"I think you will find, Mr. Feltham, that no lawyer can help you to answer questions. The best he can do is to advise you to delay your answers to another time and place, and to tell you that you have no need to answer. But it depends a little, does it not, whether your aim is to help the police to solve this crime, or whether you only want to save yourself embarrassment?"

His words had a visible effect on Feltham, as he hoped they would. But then, no intelligent man would refuse an appeal couched in those terms. Even if he had no intention of telling the whole truth, he would make it seem he had.

"I will tell you how and why Caroline was here last night," Feltham said, "and the unfortunate way she left. But you must allow me to give you the full reasons for these things as I go along. Without them, the bare facts would give entirely the wrong impression, and so you can't have one without the other. You must take down my story as a whole, and on the understanding that it is to be seen as a whole, and not used, as I believe the police are sometimes inclined to do in court, in the shape of damaging extracts."

Brentford looked at his watch. He was surprised and even shocked to see that it was in fact half an hour before noon. Where did the time go?

"I myself will see your statement in that way, Mr. Feltham. But I cannot answer for how others will see it, nor have I any control over what a judge may do in court."

With that, Feltham had to be content.

"At least there is one thing to be said in my favour," Feltham said. "No one has known Caroline Silcrest longer than I have. And I include her parents. For in my capacity as consultant gynaecologist at the nursing home where she was born, I was the first to see her, and I brought her into this world."

It was unexpected. Brentford might have guessed something of the sort, for he knew that Feltham and the Silcrests were acquainted, but he had not. He had assumed they were just neighbours.

He tried to think of the implications of what Feltham had said. It was not quite so much an indication of innocence as Feltham thought it was. On the contrary, as Brentford knew well, the more, the better and the longer people had known one another, the more inclined they were to murder them. It was not for nothing that the statisticians who compiled the figures had invented the phrase that 'murder is a family crime'. Except in cases of violent theft and rape, it very often was.

"So you knew the Silcrests before you came down here?" he said.

He was able to hear Feltham, who was presumably more aware of surgical statistics than police ones, piling up inferential evidence against himself.

"Yes. Professionally at first. It was the custom of the nursing home, when a birth showed signs of being difficult, to refer the case to me at an early stage. Helen Silcrest was such a case. I saw her several times before the birth, and we had to warn her that my services would probably be necessary when the time came. She was not what I would call a phlegmatic woman. Too spoiled by her beauty perhaps, and inclined to think that everything connected with her should be perfect, easy and straightforward. It was a shock to her to realise that it would not, and that she was in actual danger. I met the husband too, when he came to tell me about the distress of his wife. I did my best to reassure them both, and in the course of conversation we discovered we had several mutual acquaintances. It was not very remarkable, since my work as a surgeon, and his as a successful estate agent dealing with better properties, brought us both into contact with a large proportion of people of a certain income group. We made what I might describe as social contact. And later, when Caroline Silcrest as a child began to demonstrate that she herself was about as abnormal as her birth had been, I took an interest in the case at least as far as advising which children's doctors and psychiatrists they ought to see. Of course they thought that Caroline's behaviour

67

had something to do with her birth, and I spent quite a lot of time explaining that it had not, but was probably due to genetic or other factors."

"Just a moment," Brentford said. "You are describing Caroline Silcrest as 'abnormal'?"

He sidestepped Feltham's astonishing irrelevance.

Feltham looked surprised: "Your inquiries about Caroline can't have taken you very far, Inspector, if you have not heard that Caroline, despite inheriting her mother's beauty, was a wild and sometimes recklessly behaved child."

"Yes, I had heard she was bad," Brentford said. "But I took that just to refer to her character as a spoiled and pretty girl. You seemed to be using 'abnormal' in quite a different way. You mentioned a psychiatrist."

Feltham looked at Brentford as at an intelligent man who had still much to learn.

"It takes a psychiatrist," he said, "to say why a girl of moderately wealthy parents, with all the advantages, and certainly no lack of money or things of her own, should be found to have gone round the coats of her friends in the cloakroom at school, and stolen things from their pockets which were later found in her possession. I don't know if that is relevant to your murder case, Inspector, but it is what happened."

"I see," said Brentford. He himself did not know whether it had any relevance to his murder case or not. But he could not disregard it. In almost all cases, some kind of presumption had to be made about the character of the murdered person, if only to explain their actions or what they were doing at the time. For a moment he was inclined to chase the lead almost to the exclusion of Feltham's story.

"This kind of thing went on?" he asked.

"Naturally it varied as the girl grew older," Feltham told him. "A child does not develop static faults, like an adult. Boys who steal and cheat want to be gangsters later. It takes girls another way. They have the weaknesses and at the same time the opportunities of their sex. You may hardly believe it, but Caroline was only twelve the first time she got into trouble over a boy."

"When you say 'Got into trouble'——?"

"I said 'Got in trouble over' not 'Was got in trouble by'. It was just a reckless episode that at that age was probably confined to kissing and petting, though I have no evidence of that. But it was enough to get Caroline expelled from the rather strict school to which she had been sent, and which had agreed, not very willingly, to take her in hand after the stealing episodes."

Brentford could see his innocent murdered girl, who had looked so frail and fragile on the bank of the creek that morning, taking on a steadily more dubious light. But this, he had to remind himself, was the man, Feltham, who himself seemed to be certain, for some reason not yet clear, that he would be suspected of murdering her. He wondered if Feltham were wise to tell him these things about Caroline himself, rather than to let others do it.

"You heard of all this from the parents?" he asked. "Surely you had put it in the hands of the psychiatrist?"

"Helen Silcrest had had her second child by then," Feltham said. "Again it was a difficult birth. So difficult that I had to advise the Silcrests not to have any more children. Especially when the infant son showed very early that he was abnormal. It was obvious that there were genetic factors at work. I could not hold out any great hope to them of having a perfectly normal child. As it was, in some ways the son was a near-idiot who needed special care and attention, the provision of which came near to blighting the father's life and financial prospects. And the parents, perhaps because of the children, did not get on too well. These things happen when it is clear that one or the other has a genetic background which must cause abnormal children, especially when we could not say with certainty which of them it was. Naturally each suspected the other and developed a kind of horror of their enforced intimacy. Because it was enforced. The children were in a precarious enough state. It would have been psychological murder of the children for the parents to separate. You can imagine what would have happened to the nervous son, who needed a specially stable environment, and all the love and understanding his parents could give him, if he had had his home torn apart around him. And even the daughter. She got worse at this time. It was difficult enough to find a school that would hold her. There were odd things. Her language and wild behaviour. Bad behaviour, as though she indulged in deliberate badness. She went to and was removed from two or three schools. So George and Helen Silcrest were tied together for their children's sake. For children they could not take pride in, but for whom they had to struggle and ruin their own lives, just to keep up an appearance of normality. And I was their friend now. I could not help it, both knowing them and having been closely connected with their struggle. And besides, I had begun to take a special interest in the case of Caroline Silcrest."

Feltham seemed to be explaining unnecessarily, and Brentford watched him closely, making no secret of the intentness of his observation.

"That is why you are telling me this?" he said. "To explain the closeness of your connection with Caroline Silcrest, and the reason she was here last night?"

Feltham passed a hand over his face. It was odd that, despite his articulate intellect, he seemed to be struggling, as though there were too many complications and he had too much to say.

Brentford had the distinct impression that it was not the details, the complications that mattered, but that there was some other, vital thing, that was still unsaid.

"This does not explain why you should have taken an interest in Caroline particularly," he said, "nor why she was here last night, nor even how it happened that when the family moved here, which is what I assume must have happened, then you came here too."

"You are seeing connections when there aren't any!" Feltham said. He stirred in his chair, took a grip on himself, and continued with his narrative as though compelled by some compulsion that did not come from outside.

"I couldn't help it," he said. "I told you. By then I knew the parents. They relied on me and came back to me in a way they did not with other doctors. Just because they had known me longer, and despite the fact that my speciality was not at all what they needed now. As though I, because I had once

70

hinted that the cause of this trouble was in their genetic make-up, knew something about their children that the other doctors did not. Nothing is more difficult than not to get involved in your patients' affairs when you have known them long enough. And I was involved. I had recommended the psychiatrists and children's doctors who had advised them that, at all costs, they must keep their marriage going. And I was not sure they were right. I have told you what those doctors said, and what I myself had advised and agreed with at first. But knowing the family made me wonder. I had to get to know the family better to know if the advice that was given was really right. Despite all my other preoccupations, the problem worried me, even because it was not my subject and yet, advising on it, I had somehow become involved in it. You see, the father was erratic. Very naturally, with all this around him, he sought solace sometimes outside his home-life. There was a nurse in particular. Helen could, and probably would have divorced him, except for the advice about the children. Or he would have left her, and the children, but for the same reason. Only it was when the father was particularly attentive to this other woman, the nurse, that Caroline produced the worst example of her behaviour. It became so bad that she was sent off to a boarding school, to get her out of it. That did not make it look like a marriage that should be kept going for the children's sake. On the contrary, I began to wonder if we did not see these things the wrong way. Taking a moral point of view, as it were, instead of logic, sense and science. I wondered. I wondered too much perhaps, and all the more as I was having difficulty with my surgery at that time. The details need not concern you, but I wondered if this was not the kind of thing I should have specialised in. It was approaching the time when I decided to retire . . ."

Feltham was not quite so explicit or coherent as he had been, Brentford noticed. There were slight contradictions, too. He had said originally that he had chosen to retire. Now he was speaking of difficulties in his work, as though that retirement had not been quite, entirely, a matter of choice. But Feltham knew it, quite obviously. His expression, looking at Brentford, was one of an appeal.

"I spent time, far too much time, thinking of why Caroline Silcrest was the way she was," he said. "I wished I could devote myself to things like that, but it was too late. At nearly fifty, you can't throw up surgery and take to a study of the brain, combined with genetics and child psychology. If only for the simple reason that there's no such science! We know nothing about the subject. Who studies human character as a whole? We leave it to the novelists and playwrights."

"And so?" said Brentford. Feltham had forgotten, he noticed, that there was another profession that studied human character. And Brentford had studied it well enough to know at just what point in a narrative attempted digressions came.

Feltham dropped his voice. He spoke in a different, factual way.

"George Silcrest decided to solve his problems. They had become almost insoluble, but not quite. His son was nearing school age, but it was clear by then that he would never go to school. If they kept on as they were his wife would go mad with jealousy, his daughter would become a prostitute, and his son would go to one of those expensive private lunatic asylums, and to keep him there would take every penny that he earned. It sounds disastrous but it was so. He decided on a new break and a new start. The son could not be kept at home in the crowded circumstances of a city, among the neighbours. But he obtained, in his work, quite suddenly, an option on the land of this estate. It was not merely that if he moved here he could keep his family together, in privacy, and devote himself to them the way he should have done. But the development of the estate, which was what it amounted to, would show a handsome profit if he could achieve it. A capital gain that would leave him rent-free, with still enough to live on. He asked me, not expecting any result, if I would take over and finance one of the houses he projected building here. I said I would. I became tied to the Silcrests in another way, you see, and I wondered, both at the time and afterwards, if at least one of my motives was not to be near to, and keep in closer and more intimate touch with, the problem of Caroline Silcrest."

Feltham paused.

"It's up to you, Inspector, to ask me whatever questions you like about the involvements of my career, finance, and my own psychology," he said. "But that is the way things are in life. They are never simple, as they are represented to be. There are always too many things involved, and I can't explain it."

Brentford treated him almost gently.

"What you are telling us, Mr. Feltham, is that for a long time, over a long period, you have developed a passion, an obsession about this girl? You know that it doesn't fit in with your profession or your background, but none the less it explains both why she was here last night, and why her mother, despite the fact that the father would have disapproved, assumed at once, as soon as she was missing from home, that she was still here?"

Feltham said nothing. The expression of his tense, nervous face, was one of suffering, directed at the floor.

"You have been having the girl here, at your house, quite frequently?" Brentford said. "And, recently, at times and in circumstances that have met with the father's disapproval? And so, since she was here, and at a time when her father had explicitly told her to stay at home, and you were the last person known to have seen her alive, you assume that there will be a natural presumption on everyone's part that you were the one who murdered her?"

Feltham nodded first, and then looked up.

"It's not only that," he said.

A little to their surprise, he got up, went to the door, and looked back at them with an unmistakable invitation to them to follow him.

They got up. Once, after an equally long explanation, Brentford had been taken to a body in that way. This time, he already had a body. But he followed Feltham none the less, with Ball following him, and they went out into the hall, turned left to the staircase, and went up the stairs. Once up the stairs, Feltham turned right, to the door of a small back bedroom, and opened the door, and stood back to let them go in.

It was a small bedroom which might have been used for a girl who was one of the family, and a daughter of the house.

73

From the window, over the rise of land above the cliffs, it was possible to see the sea. And the bedroom seemed to have been inhabited. There were oddments of clothes, and shoes, and a towel, and a bathing dress laid out to dry, all of which seemed to have been in use up to some time on the previous day.

The bed was made, but covered with a coverlet, and had not been used. On it, laid neatly, but not too neatly, as though they had just been taken off with the expectation that they would soon be put on again, was a complete set of girl's clothing.

Brentford recognised them. They were the blue dress, the underclothing, the pair of white socks, of which he had obtained a description, as an afterthought, from the father. And just below the bed were the white laced shoes.

Crosston, searching the countryside for the girl's clothing, was wasting his time.

CHAPTER FIFTEEN

So this was it, Brentford thought, standing in the bedroom. This was what they had been looking for. He had stayed on the estate. He had not gone off, to set up his headquarters in Loebeach, and he had not left Ball and the other detective-sergeants and detective-constables, of whom he could command quite a number, to deal with the minor details, the interviewing of the parents and the neighbours. Instead, he had followed up the leads, while they were live, still fresh, himself. And it had led him to this, to the silent evidence of the clothes on the bed.

It was all too simple, he thought, looking at the clothes and wondering what possible error or mistake there could be. Blue dress, white shoes and socks. But murders were simple. You found a body, and then you found the clothes. You arrested the man in whose possession the clothes were found. Possession of a murdered girl's clothes was a damning piece of evidence in any trial. What people said counted little, in relation to such actual items of evidence as that. So the man was convicted, and it was a feather in your cap, and your unorthodox methods had paid off, and you were well on your way to your promotion.

He turned round and looked at Feltham, who was standing in the doorway.

"You will remember I have shown you this voluntarily, Inspector?" Feltham said. "You did not have cause to suspect or search my house. I told you she was here last night, and I brought you here myself."

Hovering in the doorway, Feltham looked relieved but anxious. Relieved perhaps because he had told them, shown them, what it was that had been on his mind since he had received his phone calls. Anxious because, even after all his explanation, which had, after all, said very little, he did not know how his revelation was going to be received.

Brentford did not look at him in any friendly way. It was all very well for Feltham to say that he had shown them the clothes voluntarily, but they had been coming to the house when he had met them. It was true he had had very little time, but even so he might either have called the police or, failing that, have told the parents.

"I gather the girl was here often," he said. He looked around the room. The bathing costume was still damp. He went across the room and touched it. Then he looked back at Feltham. "Did her parents, her father in particular, know she had a room here?"

Feltham looked more worried again. He was not happy about it despite his long friendship with the parents, despite the time he had known the girl, and despite his protestations.

"There's a lot I haven't told you yet, Inspector."

It was true there was, thought Brentford grimly. All Feltham had told them so far, it was clear, was merely background, intended to dispose their minds and set the scene. They had thought they were finished, or almost finished, with his story, but now the facts were all to come.

"All right, Mr. Feltham. Have you a key to this door?"

Brentford was forced to do his thinking quickly. There

would be a platoon of anything up to a hundred men searching for these same clothes, under Crosston's direction, now. The defect of handling the case from a police car used as a mobile office was liable to be just that lack of co-ordination that arose from the lack of proper central direction and the even flow of messages and knowledge.

"Ball——" he began to say as Feltham showed him a key in the bedroom door. Out in the passage again, he closed the door and locked it, noticing that the key turned easily, as though the girl had kept her possessions privately and used the room as a second home. He put the key in his own pocket and motioned Feltham to go down the stairs again.

"You want a message through to Crosston?" Ball said.

"No." Brentford had had second thoughts about that. The presence of the clothes in the room, and the fact that Feltham had shown them to them, had certain implications. "We will wait a moment."

They went down the stairs again, and back into the flower-filled living-room where they had been.

"Now. Mr. Feltham."

Feltham had sat down again, as though he were going to resume his narrative and go on as he had done before.

"I told you how it was I had an interest in Caroline——" he said.

Brentford and Ball had remained standing. "Shall we talk about the clothes first?" Brentford said.

Feltham winced. If he did not look positively afraid, he had a very noticeable reluctance to talk about the salient facts.

His reluctance and reservations were more noticeable now, now they knew the kind of thing his story must come to in the end. Previously it had seemed to be just the story of an acquaintance, and only his own manner had indicated that there was more to come.

"I have told you, Inspector," he said with an appeal which would have been greater had it not been lessened by his obvious caution. "Caroline was here last night. I am coming to how she left again. I told you I must explain——"

"No," said Brentford.

Feltham looked at him and said nothing and was in danger of drying up altogether, into that state of mind in which witnesses gave only defensive answers to demanding questions. Brentford saw the danger and thought quickly.

"We have work to do, Mr. Feltham. You must understand that. There are some facts we must know at once. As it is, you have delayed us. Is that something you appreciate?"

Feltham nodded and looked away. He did not have to say that he had to defend himself.

"I want you to tell us how Caroline was dressed when she left here last night," Brentford said. "You can continue your explanation afterwards."

Ball looked at him silently and doubtfully, but Brentford took no notice of that.

"You have seen her clothes," Feltham said. "That is it——"

"Mr. Feltham," said Brentford, "did Caroline leave here stark naked?"

He achieved the result he expected, of shocking Feltham. He looked up sharply.

"No——!"

"Then," said Brentford with effortful patience, "what did she wear?"

Feltham looked away again. He said: "A nightdress . . ."

Sometimes, Brentford thought quietly, looking at him, the explanation was as bad, and raised more questions, than that which was explained.

"All right, Mr. Feltham," he said. "We will now have a description of that nightdress."

Feltham seemed to shrink. He had not been acting before. He truly had much to explain.

"Silk," he said in a low but precise voice. "Probably not real silk, but pink and light, and—transparent."

He had a capacity for saving himself by a word, even a damaging word, that still gave him the appearance or implication of concealing nothing.

Which did not lessen the impact of his story that the girl had been in, and then had actually left the house in such a garment.

"Right, Mr. Feltham. Silk. Pale pink. A light, semi-transparent nightdress. Anything else? Barefoot? What time was this?"

Feltham had fixed his eyes on the middle distance and seemed to contemplate something there.

"No, not barefoot. I am trying to think. A pair of white . . . I think they were sandals."

"The time?"

"The circumstances—Inspector, the circumstances were such I was distressed. I don't know if I can be sure about the time."

"We have to try to trace the movements of the girl, Mr. Feltham."

"I believe it was nearly midnight. I can't be sure. If you give me time to think——"

Brentford turned away from him to Ball. The question of the time would come up again, but he said to Ball: "Slip out and pass that description to Crosston."

He watched Ball go to pass the message through the driver and the radio that Crosston, instead of looking for clothes, should look for a nightdress now.

Then he sat down heavily in a chair.

Feltham looked at him and looked away.

"You understand now why I have so much to explain, Inspector."

"Yes, Mr. Feltham," said Brentford dryly. "I think you had better begin explaining."

Feltham gave him a questioning, anxious look.

"I suppose you think I was talking too much about other things."

Brentford thought about it. Feltham had, in fact, delayed them. He should have shown them the clothes first. But would they have listened so well if he had? Feltham had known what he was doing.

Which in itself might mean one thing or the other. It was almost impossible for a policeman to decide.

"All right, Mr. Feltham. Go on with your explanation."

"Do I understand you want me just to stick to the facts now? Only major facts?"

Brentford thought about that too.

78

"No. It was earlier you should have been shorter. Now you had better tell us everything."

"There is so much, Inspector." Feltham himself seemed to quail.

"I want to know in detail," Brentford said, "from where you left off."

And it had better be good, he thought. It had had to be good before. Now, for Feltham to extricate himself, it would have to be a masterpiece of testimony.

Feltham brooded for a moment, then he said, "I think I was telling you about George and Helen Silcrest."

Brentford at once wanted to say: "No. Tell me about yourself and Caroline", but he restrained it. He had asked for everything, and a suspect should, must, be allowed to talk.

"I mean in relation to Caroline's home-life," Feltham said. "It was what you would normally say, that the parents should stay married for the sake of the children. I don't know. When the homelife is one of deceit, jealousy ... What I am trying to tell you is that they were circumstances in which I tried to help, to show a little understanding."

If it were true, Brentford thought, and everyone would say the evidence was against it, then Feltham's understanding had got him into a rare situation.

"You claim you acted throughout as a friend of the family?"

He wanted to get it clear in familiar terms. Feltham's language had a tendency to obscurity and jargon that did not help his case in the least.

"If you like to put it like that. What I said was that I tried to exercise understanding with the girl. I am telling you why I frequently had her here. Even in the worst cases, I believed, it is remarkable what you can do with understanding."

It was, in a fashion, an explanation. Brentford thought himself into it. It was right and yet it was not right. Since he had seen the clothes and heard of the nightdress, he was not so willing to accept explanations that would have been good before. He spoke deliberately:

"In all honesty, Mr. Feltham, would you say, or not, that you fell in love with Caroline Silcrest?"

He expected a reaction from Feltham, and he got it. It took a simple person to answer a question like that directly, and Feltham was not simple. Brentford got no more than he had expected when, with considerable care and forethought, he had asked the question.

"Good heavens, Inspector, Caroline was not yet in her teens at the time we came here! If you think that she at eleven, and I, a man of forty-five——!"

Feltham sounded indignant, angry when he started, and then he stopped. His expression changed. He looked at Brentford.

"Well?" said Brentford dryly.

"You are thinking in terms of the book *Lolita*," said Feltham.

It was impossible to guess why he said just that.

Without comment, Brentford said: "You know it?"

Feltham looked at him oddly, then nodded.

"It means something to you," Brentford said.

Feltham looked as though that particular story could not fail to mean something to someone in his situation. But Brentford, watching, felt there was something more.

Feltham said: "It was——" then changed his mind.

"There was nothing like that between Caroline and myself," he said. "I am not that kind of person."

Brentford wondered silently about a girl in a nightdress being in his house at nearly midnight, which gave her very little time to be murdered even if what he said was true. Then there were the clothes and the other articles in her room.

He wondered just how to put it.

"Nothing like love?" he said. He adopted a carefully neutral tone. "Of any kind?"

Feltham had seemed absorbed since he had mentioned the book *Lolita*. He had looked away from Brentford and for a moment seemed to be concerned with some problem of his own. It did not seem to Brentford to be the time for the man to be absorbed in private problems, but it was a moment before he pulled himself together and turned to answer.

Ball slipped quietly back into the room at that point, making as little disturbance as possible and blinking a little to adjust his eyes to the cool light of the room after the sunlight outside, as he silently took out his notebook.

He must have found it odd to discover Feltham and Brentford talking about love.

"I suppose you are speaking of carnal love," said Feltham.

Brentford said gently: "You should know, Mr. Feltham. Is there any other kind?"

"Affection..." said Feltham dryly. Then: "I have noticed that Christians who speak of pure and selfless love never seem to believe in it. Perhaps if I defined my attitude as a more scientific interest, and curiosity..." He seemed to force himself forward with an effort: "Whatever it was, against a background of Caroline coming to my house on the way to the beach each day, I was succeeding."

Brentford glanced at Ball and said: "Succeeding?"

Feltham considered what he had to say.

"Take the matter of her clothes. You can't understand, of course, not knowing Caroline. She was an exhibitionist. Not merely in the shape of tantrums, though I had enough of those. I mean something more deliberate. When she discovered this was a private estate to which her parents had brought her, she took advantage of it. She would run around the estate, and past my house and to and from the beach, in a state in which it would have been impossible for her to appear on the public streets. At first I thought it was just wildness, and it probably was. But I saw fairly rapidly that it was not innocent. A matter of where she changed her clothes. I would come across her far too often accidentally in the nude. I made a point of making it clear to her that, as a doctor, that certainly did not affect me. I gave her the room in the house to change in, and suggested to her that, since it was a private estate, to sunbathe in the nude on the beach was quite all right. She was not accustomed to such treatment. Instead of scolding her, I let her see that nothing she did was quite as shocking as she thought it was. When I was able to talk to her about such things, I remarked that a woman in clothes, the right clothes, was far more affecting to a man than one without. Then I chanced to take her with me in the car to town and let her buy things of which her parents would probably not approve, but which did at least represent the beginning of some kind of rudimentary taste or sense of some kind. I do not say I succeeded in getting her to a normal girl's attitude to clothes, but I was succeeding. She had begun to regard them as a personal adornment, and not as an unwelcome necessity forced on her by other people from the outside."

Brentford tried to understand a situation in which, if he could believe it, such a step was regarded as a success, an advance.

But he looked at Feltham narrowly and asked him a personal question.

"And did she appreciate this?" he said. "It went on for some time, this kind of thing. Did she understand your attitude, in fact, and what you were trying to do for her?"

There were more implications in the question than appeared on the surface, and Feltham seemed to understand them.

He looked at Brentford steadily and in silence for a moment, and then he said:

"You don't expect that kind of reward from a girl like Caroline. I have already told you that her attitude to me differed little from her antagonism to other people. It seemed to make very little difference that I tolerated her and others didn't. The way she repaid me was the kind of thing you would expect. I know what you will think of this, in view of everything else, but one day she went to her father and told him calmly I had tried to rape her."

Brentford felt his responsibilities weighing on him.

He realised that his case against Feltham, if he in his position decided to bring one, was quite complete.

CHAPTER SIXTEEN

Feltham saw what was passing in Brentford's mind. He paled a little, looked out of the window at the estate, and back.

He sat very still in his chair. He said: "People will tell you that. To make you believe me, I can only tell you that was Caroline. You must check my story. When she discovered it was possible, she didn't only make that allegation against me, but against other people."

Brentford did not look at Ball. He knew that that statement would be taken down verbatim.

And it was in accordance with what Feltham had been telling them from the start, that everything was explicable in terms of the character of the dead girl.

If, that was, that was believable. Brentford had never found the character of the one who was murdered feature quite so large before. He had chanced to say she was still alive, but he had not thought to that extent.

His policeman's question was inevitable: "Who did she accuse?"

Feltham was unwilling. For once he looked around as though he would rather be anywhere than where he was Then he said: "William Morris."

Brentford looked at him steadily and said: "And now you had better come to the point and tell us what happened here last night."

"You will confirm that she did accuse others?"

Brentford did not say yes or no. He said: "About last night, Mr. Feltham."

Feltham looked out at the full post-noon sunlight on the lawn outside the window. He said:

"I wanted to tell you why her father reacted particularly to her stories about me. It is probably not right or proper to say he was jealous of my association with Caroline. I don't think he thought of it in those terms. For years he had been quite willing and eager that I should take an interest in Caroline, and he was quite aware that she was seeing me and that she should regard this house as her second home. But he did begin to feel it, I think, when my methods began to have some success with her and his didn't."

Brentford remembered what Silcrest had said about Feltham. Feltham might think he was anticipating again what they were going to hear, but if so, this time, he was wrong. They had already heard it.

"So there is that too," he said. "You and Mr. Silcrest had a disagreement about his daughter."

Feltham looked like a man who was hedged in with difficulties every way he turned.

"She had grown older," he said. He gave the impression of being carefully just to Silcrest. "If you look at it that way, it was one thing for her to come here every day, and for me to talk to her, and for her even to spend an occasional night here, as she did on rare occasions, when she was eleven or twelve. When she was fourteen and fifteen it was different. She was different. She made trouble deliberately by talking to him about her love-life and, over the matter of the clothes, referring to me as her sugar-daddy."

Brentford had to resist the fascinated inclination to pursue it.

If it was true, it was staggering, what Feltham had endured for the sake of the girl. According to Feltham, her attitude had been positively vicious, with every intention of creating the maximum amount of trouble between the man who had befriended her and her father. And yet, if it were true, he had gone on seeing her.

It raised problems of whether it was believable.

He said again, patiently: "About last night, Mr. Feltham . . ."

It was not his business to check a witness, but to let him go on and on. Usually, that worked. The most loquacious speaker dried up sooner or later and made way for the insistent question. But Feltham had obviously little conception of Superintendent Crawford, or of how the Chief Constable of the county himself would shortly become dissatisfied with the receipt of bodies, bereaved fathers, and now clothes, without any explanation of what was happening in a case that must, by now, be the subject of endless questions from the press. He doubted if Feltham had even thought of the press yet.

Feltham had looked quickly away from him, struggling.

Yet he had to come to it.

Brentford repeated, with a patience that seemed inhuman to Ball: "What did happen yesterday, Mr. Feltham?"

Feltham turned to him abruptly and looked full at him. He seemed to summon up his energy and will-power.

He said: "We quarrelled about *Lolita*."

Brentford looked at him silently. He had wondered why Feltham had mentioned *Lolita* before.

Then he tried to imagine it. That girl and that man quarrelling about that particular book, which must have had a violent significance to both of them.

It almost convinced him that it was true, after all the story, the sheer inevitability of it.

As it was, he neither laughed nor raised his voice. He just looked at Feltham and breathed a little harder.

"Mr. Feltham," he said, "I should think you would. Quarrel about that book."

But Feltham took it seriously, looking at Brentford with bitter eyes.

"You asked me," he said. "That was the beginning of it. I'm telling you, Inspector."

"Go on," said Brentford.

Feltham looked away again.

"She got it from my library. I want to be quite clear. If I am not, you will ask me for further details. This was in the afternoon. It was not that she visited me exactly with her parents knowledge and consent, though they hardly made any attempt to stop it. Caroline herself saw to that, and there was nothing they could do about it short of locking her permanently in her room. And you can see what the situation is. The sea beach lies behind my house, and they could not keep her away from that. She simply called, as she always had, no matter what anyone said. She would come into my house without asking and go up to what she regarded as her room.

She kept her swimming costume and towel and beach things there, and I had not brought myself to the stage of locking her out."

"In other words you continued to receive her," Brentford said.

"I would see her on the beach anyway. In good weather like the present I would go there myself. Usually we would be the only two people on the beach. It was pointless to keep her out of the house."

"Go on."

"So she called at the house, as she regularly did, as she had been doing all the summer. She went to pick up her things and asked me if I was coming down. I said I was, and went to get ready. That was when she got the book. During the ten or twenty minutes she was in the house, she went to my book-shelves and picked up something to read. It was not until we were going down to the beach that I saw she was carrying the copy of *Lolita*. I was annoyed. I had put it behind the other books and out of sight, in a place where I had thought she would not find it. I stopped her and asked her to take it back and not to read it."

Brentford stopped him: "What exactly did you say?" he said.

Feltham looked at him hopefully. "I said: 'You know I always give you free run of my shelves, but that book is particularly offensive in view of the situation of the two of us.' She said: 'Do you think I haven't heard of it, that I don't know what it is?' I said: 'Heaven knows, Carol, that there's nothing that I think you too young to know, or that there's anything you don't know. But this is a matter of taste, my taste. I shall find it objectionable to see you read that book.' And she said: 'You're ashamed, aren't you? You don't want me to know what you felt like when we were as we were a few years ago.'"

Brentford looked at Feltham grimly, and then at the clock, which had moved on and was showing twenty-five to two. There were so many implications or possible implications in the exchange that Feltham had given him that he could not hope to trace them.

"You both went back?" he said, prompting.

"No. I knew better than to insist with Caroline. When she believed she could see a weakness in an older person, she would do her utmost to exploit it. It was better to let her have the book. It certainly would not tell her anything she did not know. I tried to appear indifferent."

Feltham seemed to indicate that he had highly-evolved mental processes for dealing with the bad child, and he gave them a glimpse of what they were.

"But you did not succeed?" said Brentford.

"She did not allow me to succeed. We went down to the beach in the usual way. She went for a swim, and came back to read the book. At least she read parts of it from somewhere around the middle, which she knew was a practice I found annoying. She looked up at me and said: 'Uncle,'—it is odd, but she kept that name for me from childhood—'Why didn't you make love to me, a few years ago, when I was younger and would have been more excited about it and you knew you had the chance?' I said: 'I should have done. I should have seduced you while you were still a virgin, if you can think back as far as that, and put you out of my mind, instead of putting up with you the way you are at present.' I wanted to shock her."

Feltham showed no embarrassment, nor any expectation of shocking as he told Brentford of the exchanges.

Brentford looked at him steadily as though it were every day of his life that he heard a man of fifty on those terms with a young girl.

"You said you quarrelled," he said.

"We were already quarrelling! About the book. I was not in the habit of criticising Caroline. It would have been impossible for me to have any influence on her if I had been. You notice I was saying things she need not necessarily take seriously, though she, I knew, was serious. That was the only kind of criticism you could make with a girl like her, to say exaggeratedly hard things as though you did not mean them. But she said: 'You're a pretty sick man, aren't you, Uncle? Is a fixation on young girls senility or just some weakness that made you never marry?' I said: 'What gives you the wish to make everyone hate you, including me?' And before we knew where we were, we had a flaming row."

Brentford frowned sharply: "Was this kind of thing normal in your relations with Caroline?"

"No, on the contrary, it was quite exceptional. What she had said struck home, you see. It was ridiculous, but in my absorbtion with her I had never realised that she saw me in quite that light. I was like a parent who had not realised a child was growing up, except that in her case her parents had realised it, while I had not. I felt angry. There was nothing wrong with that. A little healthy anger, from the person they have injured, does nothing but good with girls like Caroline. Only instead of saying the things that I knew would affect her, which was my usual way, I found I was speaking my mind outright. Treating her as an adult, an equal you understand, which was absurd. I said: 'Caroline, I have wasted five years of my life on you. I don't regret it. At least it was worth a try. But if you are not now capable of the least sign of respect or gratitude, I will have to acknowledge that I have failed, and I am through with you!' She laughed, happy that she had been successful, and said: 'Uncle, Uncle, if you knew how silly you look when you look like that!' She was like a stupid gleeful child, which was a thing I had been able to excuse in the past because she was a child. But she was no child now. I got up from the beach and left her."

"This was in the afternoon?" said Brentford.

"Yes, this was in the afternoon. I went back to the house and changed. Then I went out. I did not want to meet her when she came back. I wanted her to know that I had meant what I said."

"It is the evening we want to know about."

"Yes, I understand that. But I did not come back in the evening until quite late. I was making up my mind, you see. Caroline, I imagined, had thought that I was joking. But I decided that I was not. George Silcrest's changed attitude to me had had its effect, though I had not known it at the time. I was suddenly seeing that I was giving more and more to Caroline and getting less and less. She was of an age now when people really would suspect that there was something

88

between us. Not that I had let that affect me before. A man in my position doesn't take a great deal of notice of what people think. But if it was in her eyes that I appeared an old fool, a dotard, then I realised it would not do. I was surprised how pained I felt. I began to feel shocked how painful I found it. It was unexpected. But I persisted, and had dinner out. I was afraid to go back because she might wait at the house and expect me. We had had tiffs before that ended in that way, but I felt this was too serious."

Feltham looked at Brentford with a new, pained expression and said: "I stayed out until ten o'clock, Inspector, and then came back here, to what I presumed was an empty house."

Simply, and because it had to be that way, Brentford said: "It wasn't?"

But Feltham's eyes had left his and were looking round the room. He identified what it was. He said: "The flowers."

They had not realised that the flowers which filled the room, which they had seen when they came in, were so important.

It seemed they were. Looking at them, Feltham's lips parted before he began to speak, and then he looked at Brentford.

"I was not lying to you when I said that the inside of this house is not usually like this. But it was, lighted and like this, when I got back. And apparently empty." He looked around the room again. "There was a fire, and my slippers were laid beside it. But the room was empty. I could only assume that she had done all this for me and then gone home."

Brentford felt something in Feltham he had not sensed before. It was the empty loneliness of a bachelor of increasing age.

Perhaps it was because at that point Feltham began to lose his competent articulate air.

"You probably don't understand ... Caroline had never done anything like this before. So far as I knew for anyone. She was not a girl for housework. I came in here and sat by the fire and put on the slippers she had laid out, looked at the flowers, and thought about it. I realised what I had been feeling in the afternoon. You spoke of love ... It was not what I expected, to discover I had such an affection for her. And I was sitting there, in the position you can see, in the chair with the back to the door."

Feltham looked down at the floor of the room. He had indicated the flowers in the vases, the ashes of the hearth, and the chair. But he avoided looking at either Ball or Brentford.

"I heard a sound behind me," he said.

He looked up at Brentford with an effort.

"She was there. She had been in the house. In her room. Waiting, I presume. But I can't express it. The difference between what I was thinking and what I saw. Except that for a moment I was not sure."

"What do you mean, you weren't sure?" said Brentford.

Feltham looked at Brentford as though he wondered if he would understand.

"She came in, towards me. She was wearing that nightdress I told you of."

He himself looked as though there were something he did not understand, or feared as he silently compared the vision of the girl in the nightdress and the purpose for which he had described it to Brentford.

"She was made up ... I don't know if you understand how it is when a young girl is made up. It gives them a look, especially wearing a garment like that."

He moved restlessly in his chair.

"But she just came in," he said sharply. He controlled his voice with difficulty: "What I saw was that she had made herself as beautiful as she was able. And with the light shining through that nightdress she was beautiful. I could have seen it as a picture. To add to my confusion she came in silently, not her usual way, and knelt beside me. Then she spoke. She said 'David.' She did not normally call me David."

Feltham's face contorted. "She said: 'David, don't let's deceive ourselves any longer! Please don't! I've made the bed.'"

Feltham got up from his chair and turned away to the window, to stand with his back to them.

It was a moment before he said: "I reacted."

Brentford gave him a moment before he said:

"What do you mean, you reacted, Mr. Feltham?"

Feltham turned to them.

"I was angry, furious, you understand?" His face expressed the words as though he were living the emotion then. "It was—— She had said it so innocently. And yet we were right back where we had been that afternoon. But worse, because she meant it. Can you understand that, a girl of her age, speaking to me? You understand the difficulty I have had telling this to you? She was asking me to go to bed with her! How do you think that I reacted?"

Brentford watched him for a moment and then said evenly: "Mr. Feltham, I am asking you what happened."

Feltham looked at him as though he should know it, as though he should not have to say it.

"I told her what she was, of course——!" His expression changed as he said it. He looked at the flowers and put his hands to his face. "God, I—— You know why I asked if it was suicide! I told her to get out, and she didn't. I began to tear her character apart——" He looked at the rug before the hearth, with its dead fire of ashes. "I had pushed her away from me. She was lying there. She began to answer me back."

Watching him, Brentford wondered if the man knew what he was saying. If he was acting a part, it was not merely consummate acting, but he was sailing dangerously close to the wind.

Without putting any emphasis on the words, he said: "In fact you had a violent quarrel."

Feltham stopped and looked at him. For a moment he looked afraid.

"I told you I told her to get out. And in the end she did. I threw her out."

Feltham was still standing in the direction of the window, and Brentford saw a movement behind him. It was in the distance, across the garden. It was someone coming in the direction of the house, and Brentford knew his time was iimited. He looked past Feltham and out through the window for a moment.

The movement was their driver. But he was coming up the path, and, behind him, in the greater distance, there was a car moving up the drive.

"But this went on some time," he said. He transferred his attention back to Feltham.

Feltham seemed to shrink again. "Yes, this went on some

91

time. We knew one another well! There were things we could say. It's true to say we quarrelled..."

Brentford studied him. So this was it, he thought. It happened. The story and the man you either believed or did not believe. And this was the account that was to explain Feltham's manner, the clothes, the room, the presence of the girl at that hour, and—her departure?

"And you say you threw her out?" he said. "What do you mean by that?"

It was a neutral tone asking about words.

Feltham looked at him stupidly none-the-less, with the view behind him through the window of the driver coming up the path and the second car arriving now.

"I mean them literally," he said. "I—I could do nothing else. I threw or pushed or dragged her out."

He shuddered in his standing position.

Brentford watched him closely, wondering if he should have him sit down first. He said: "As she was? You didn't have her dress first?"

Feltham stared at him for a moment.

"Naturally, one of the first things I had told her was to get dressed!"

"She wouldn't?"

"I got her out of this room, dragging her to the hall. I told her to go up and dress. She wouldn't! You have to understand that. She wouldn't do anything I said! I couldn't force her up the stairs and dress her! Truly, Inspector——! I pulled her to the front door. That was all I could do. This is a private estate." Feltham looked ghastly. He turned sharply away again:

"I presumed she would get home all right."

Brentford looked at the man's back, wondering if a man who had murdered a girl could say that just like that.

It was the weight of his office to be expected to know such things, and then and there, on the spot, he didn't.

It was like falling back and choosing the lesser role, to say: "What time was this?"

It was a question a constable was taught to ask, and told to write down the answer.

Feltham turned and looked at him as though he saw him.

At the same time trying to think.

"I looked at the clock at some time. If I can't remember? It was twenty to twelve I think..." He might have said more or qualified it in some way.

Feltham was interrupted by the hammering of the driver on the door.

CHAPTER SEVENTEEN

Practical considerations supervened. They usually did, no matter what or for whom the personal crisis. Even an Inspector in charge of a murder case could not expect to remain serenely alone with his victims indefinitely.

"A message for the Inspector," the driver was saying firmly to Ball, who had gone to the door to ask him, in a subdued voice that penetrated, what the hell he wanted.

Brentford looked at Feltham, who was looking distraught, very naturally, and at his wits' end inevitably, but perhaps, Brentford thought, not quite so distraught and at his wits' end as he might have been.

A difficult point, that.

"What is it?" Ball was saying impatiently.

"From the Superintendent; for the Inspector," the driver said obstinately.

"That is all I know," said Feltham. He was listening to Ball and the driver with apparent relief at the fortuitous interruption.

Brentford thought quite clearly: the astonishing thing is that I almost believe him. And then he thought: or do I?

"Well, damn it, what is the message?"

"Personal——"

"He won't thank you if you interrupt him..." Ball's voice faded.

Through the blinds across the window it was easy to see

why, in the shape of Crosston arriving in his car and starting, with a young army of men behind him, across the lawn.

Brentford was due to be interrupted anyway.

"The Super sends his courteous regards to the Inspector, and will he please have lunch with him," the driver said.

"Lunch——?" Ball's voice had an expression as he said the word. At first, Brentford thought it was indignation that such an item should be allowed to interrupt Feltham's statement.

Then Brentford realised it wasn't. It was Ball's feeling for the importance of the message: since it was about something that he, never mind what Brentford thought, still regarded as important.

"So much for loyalty," Brentford said silently in his mind.

"I suppose you will want to arrest me now?"

"I don't think so, quite, just yet." Brentford tried to sound reassuring but only succeeded in sounding preoccupied.

Lunch with the Superintendent was not just lunch. It was virtually a royal command. It was what happened when a Superintendent thought a case was not proceeding satisfactorily.

It was a way the Superintendent had of putting in a personal appearance on a case. Not asking for a personal full report, or setting up an Inquiry, but just having lunch with the Inspector on the spot.

"At the Golden Arms," the driver was telling Ball as though that were vital information.

"Or will you take me in for questioning?" Feltham said.

Brentford had told the Superintendent, Superintendent Crawford, whose similarity to Brentford's own name signified no similarity of temperament, that he was expecting an early arrest. It had been intended to keep Crawford quiet. Now he had a chance to make one.

He must keep a sense of proportion.

"No, Mr. Feltham. Just don't leave your house or go away...."

It was unfortunately true that you needed time, sometimes quite a lot of time, to check the alleged facts of a statement before you brought the man in to question him on it.

94

"Ball!" It was Crosston's voice now. Apparently he was nearing the door. "What the hell is going on here?"

Crosston sounded cheerful, almost. At least current events were not his responsibility.

Brentford gave up the hope of getting more from Feltham at present. He went to the door. Feltham stayed in the room, listening no doubt.

"A message from the Superintendent, sir——" the driver began to say.

"Look, John." Crosston did not sound as cheerful with Brentford as he had with Ball. "This business about a night-dress. There's a whole square mile of woods here. Do you really mean it? Because if you do, we need the Army——"

"Come in," said Brentford. He did not like the question about the Army. That was the way it was. Perhaps they did not have a hundred men. On the spur of the moment, with the Superintendent waiting (he must actually be at the Golden Arms), he had to decide whether Feltham's story were true enough to call out the Army.

He felt in his pocket, took out and pressed a key into Crosston's hand. "The small back bedroom," he told him earnestly, in the same reassuring voice he had used with Feltham. "The original clothes are in it——"

Crosston was in, glancing about significantly. He saw the partly open door to the living room as Brentford indicated it with a gesture.

"You have someone in there? He is the one——?" he dropped his voice.

"You don't need the Army, Arthur."

"It sounds like the one chance of lunch we'll get," Ball was saying to the driver.

"Shall we come in, sir?" one of Crosston's men was saying to Crosston.

Brentford thought of an army detachment searching the woods in response to Feltham's story, and of what someone, say Crawford, would say of it. Yet he almost believed Feltham. Almost. Or almost thought he did. "With the men you have," he said. "On a straight line, say, from here to the creek. On the drives, and if there are any footpaths——"

He tried to visualise a girl walking through the woods at midnight in a nightdress, and wondered if he believed in her. But she had been real enough on the beach.

He started Crosston on a new tack. If anyone called out the Army, it would have to be Crosston on Crosston's responsibility. He gestured, after glancing at the filling hall, to the partly open door.

"About him," he said.

"Yes, what do we do about him?" Crosston's eyes came up alert. He sniffed as though he smelled something. After a morning's work, his spirit was still undimmed.

"Don't question him too much," Brentford said quickly, and dropped his voice. Feltham could probably overhear. "Find out which way the girl went ... If you need any help, you'll probably get me at the Golden Arms ... Don't give him a chance to rehearse his story..."

Brentford made up his mind and edged strategically to the door.

It was not true that he was abdicating the situation, he thought. It was too bad about Feltham in Crosston's hands. But if the man did have the dead girl's clothes in his house... He had a good excuse, a reason almost, in the shape of the royal command from Crawford.

"If you once get involved, you'll find it takes two hours, and if it exists I want that nightdress."

He was pushing out through the door, where Ball and the driver waited.

"Look, John——!" said Crosston in sudden alarm.

"Good luck," said Brentford firmly.

He ought to say good-bye or something more to Feltham, he thought as he headed down the path. He didn't. Feltham, whether his story were true, or not, was in a way beyond redemption, the way people were in a case of murder.

"The Superintendent says will you please have lunch with him at the Golden Arms," the driver said. With an air of injustice, knowing he would be blamed for it (or what were drivers and messengers for?), he said : "It's getting late."

"I know," said Brentford, looked back at the Feltham house, and went with them thoughtfully to the car.

CHAPTER EIGHTEEN

The case was dead for a while. Superintendent Crawford had lunched alone, at a table by a low window in the long, low-beamed, first-storey dining room. Brentford, he thought. Their names were sufficiently alike for him to feel responsible for Brentford, though there was no justice in the feeling, and so far he had a very confused picture of the case. It was a case which had attracted the Chief Constable's notice, and that was the reason he was there.

Damn Brentford, he thought, looking out at the view of the bay and the rivermouth beyond the Loebeach beach. "Age fifteen" and "body unclothed" the preliminary reports said, and everyone knew what that meant. The national dailies would take an interest, the national dailies which, concentrating on London, normally left the outer counties to live in the peaceful obscurity of unknown rural England. And Chief Constables were sensitive to the national dailies. That was the point at which it was not what you did but what you were seen to do that mattered.

Damn Brentford, he thought, for being inaccessible, uncertain and erratic on just the one case—— He saw Brentford's arrival with relief.

That was what was "wrong" with Brentford. You felt relief when he did the obvious thing, such as arriving when you sent a message for him. There was that uneasiness. With another man you never even wondered if maybe he wouldn't. "Sit down, John," he said. "You've got a fine day for your case at least." He was grimly polite and helpful.

He pointed to the chair opposite to him across his table as though this were just a minor matter, in which he took a paternal interest, but Brentford was not deceived.

"It's a bad one, sir," he said abruptly. "Have you got the doctor's report yet on whether the girl was raped or not?" He was looking round as he spoke to see that the waiters and other people were out of earshot.

Crawford stared at him. "You mean there's any doubt it's that kind of case?"

"That's it. The doctor seemed doubtful in the first place." In the two minutes while he sat at the table before the waiter arrived, Brentford acquainted Crawford with the doctor's inability to find superficial signs of rape, with the position of the body, and the minor indications that had led him to seek its immediate origin on the estate.

"You could have sent a local uniformed constable to make inquiries," Crawford said promptly, interrupting coldly.

It was true enough, Brentford thought while the waiter came to take his order. A uniformed constable, inquiring whether any girls were missing, would have obtained positive results at the second house he came to. The fact that he would not have seen Helen Silcrest's arrival at the Morrises was neither here nor there. It was not proved yet that anything Brentford had seen then was of the slightest value.

"I'll have the crab salad," he told the waiter.

"I'm afraid the crab salad's off, sir. You're rather late."

But it was not possible to describe in detail to Crawford in two minutes the detailed and complicated events which had taken all the morning. He waited until the waiter had gone with his order of cold meat and potatoes, which was apparently all that was left of the lunchtime menu, and then said: "A constable couldn't have found out for me where the girl was put into the water."

"You found that?"

"I believe so. But a constable had got there first and destroyed all the positive evidence that might have proved it, before we got there."

"Who was that, one of Crosston's men?"

Crawford was always ready to pursue a vendetta of the C.I.D. against the uniformed branch. It was his life.

"You can't expect a uniformed man looking for clues not to touch anything. If he touched nothing he'd find nothing." Brentford felt responsible for Crosston.

"What's this about you having found the clothes?"

"I acted on information received in the shape of a hint from the father."

Crawford considered that. It was unexceptionable. No one could complain if the Inspector in charge of the case followed up a hint by the dead girl's father. At the same time, if Crawford admitted it, Brentford had a good excuse for not having withdrawn to some little distance from the case and set up a local headquarters and dealt with administration in the normal way. Crawford considered the case as a whole.

"What's wrong with your man Ball? Don't you trust him to do a thing like that?"

"There's nothing wrong with Ball. It was just that it was on my way——" Brentford paused abruptly. He had been about to say: "And it was immediately obvious that Feltham would be a prime suspect in the case." But he thought better of that. "It immediately became clear that Feltham's evidence was of prime importance in tracing the movements of the girl. If I had left him to Ball and retired to a headquarters somewhere, the first thing I would have had to do would have been to call him in."

Crawford looked at the waiter appearing with Brentford's lunch.

"Feltham?" he said, uncertain of the name. "Is that the man who had the clothes?" He began to see things.

They waited until the waiter had come and gone.

"He admits he had the girl with him until around twenty minutes before midnight. When she left him, she was wearing a pink transparent nightdress." Brentford looked down at his lunch and up again. "He says."

Crawford frowned and pressed his lips together. It was difficult to condemn Brentford for having discovered such obviously vital evidence. At the same time, the way it had been done was all wrong. No means or machinery had been set up for collecting evidence. If Brentford had failed to procure a man who looked like a murderer, there would have been no possible excuse for him at all.

"He actually told you that? That he had the girl with him, undressed, last evening? What time was this?"

"He says she had left him by twenty to twelve. So far as I can gather, she was in the water and dead by one."

Crawford frowned again. It was all so perfect he was suspicious of it. He wondered why, then realised that Brentford was not sufficiently enthusiastic or proud of the story he was telling. Brentford again.

Brentford was just quietly eating his lunch like a man who still expected to be reprimanded, despite the fact that within four or five hours of the early morning discovery of the body he appeared to have solved a murder.

"You say the father told you of this? He knew about it? He suspected that this was going on?"

Brentford looked up, and Crawford had been right. He was not enthusiastic about what he was telling in the least.

"Yes. But I have a distinct impression that while the other people on the estate knew about all this, and in fact Feltham himself says one woman phoned him, warned him, it was only the father, and not the mother even, who out and told us."

Crawford looked taken aback, as well he might.

"What's behind all this? What kind of a statement did Feltham make?"

Brentford looked at him and smiled slightly, but not with humour. "It took two hours. I don't see how anyone can possibly get a copy until Ball has stayed up till midnight typing it."

"Dammit, you can tell me!" Crawford kept his patience with difficulty. "I will have to tell the Chief; he'll want to know!"

Brentford shook his head. It was singular, too, that he was not enjoying himself when he came to a point of triumph.

"In general, yes. He is an old friend of the family. Relations strained recently over the girl, but none the less he's known her literally since she was born. And he's fifty and a doctor. It's all so obvious and outrageous, and yet in another way it isn't."

Crawford stared.

"I can see why you want the doctor's report. I'll get on to him at once. It may not be rape, but if we discover she's not a virgin——"

"I'm not sure if it will help." Brentford shook his head again.

Crawford was silent. He simply waited.

"She isn't the kind of girl who would be a virgin anyway. Not much doubt about it, I'm afraid. I heard she was bad before I ever went to Feltham. He tells me she was expelled from several schools." He looked straight at Crawford. "One thing you could do for me, sir, is see if she has a record."

Crawford seemed to shrink from the case as though he would rather not touch it with a barge-pole. Or Brentford.

Brentford watched him patiently, eating his lunch in the meantime. It was such a simple case. Most murders, on the face of it, were. Admittedly, there was the small business of proving the guilty person's guilt in law. People who made an outcry about the number of murders that remained unsolved usually forgot that. But Crawford's reactions were forecastable. It was just not in the experience of the police that there was more than one suspect who was capable of the crime.

"You'll be getting that statement typed right away, and checked for detail? You're going after Feltham; as soon as you have the facts available for questioning, you'll bring him in?"

"I'm not so sure, sir."

Crawford stared blankly.

"You mean you believe his statement?"

Brentford wished he had not been asked that question. He very much wished it. But he had been asked.

"It was a rash statement. Not the kind they usually make."

"Dammit, I need a straight answer, man."

"Then yes. Against all the probabilities, I believed it." Brentford hesitated: "Some of it."

Crawford drew a breath. In the low-beamed dining room of the Golden Arms, in which they were the last customers except for a woman reading a book alone at the far end of the line of bay-view windows, he felt his journey had not been wasted.

"Then you were wrong, weren't you, John?" he said gently. "Wrong to go charging off bullheaded and mixing with the people of this estate? You should have set up your headquarters in the usual way, and concentrated on where people were, and times and places and chance encounters, and let this about Feltham, if it's irrelevant, appear in a few days' time." He controlled his voice with effort.

"Yes, sir," said Brentford.

Crawford was right, he thought. To a sergeant, to a man like Ball, or to a constable, Feltham would have said just when and how he had seen the girl last. And while there would have been immediate questions, about how the girl came to be leaving his house at that time, and dressed in that way, a regular, right-headed police inspector would not be put off by that. He would have gone on checking the movements of everyone in the district, and dealt with Feltham in his spare time.

"So you have finished with the estate as such?" Crawford said. "You'll be setting up in the school hall here?" His eyes looked dangerous. He took it for granted Brentford would do as he said: "You've been lucky, John. Enough has come out of this nonsense to justify your actions of this morning. The Chief won't take too poor a view of it. You're lucky to have come out with a whole skin."

Brentford had finished his meat and potatoes. He laid down his knife and fork. Or perhaps, since there were still some items on his plate, he had not quite finished, but he felt it safer to lay them down all the same.

"I did think," he said, as though it were a little matter, "of going personally back to the estate this afternoon."

Crawford gasped audibly. There was that about Crawford, Brentford realised. As an immediate superior, he left you in no doubt what he felt.

What was shocking was that, after a silence that lasted all the time it took the waiter to come and take Brentford's plate away in order to bring the sweet, his voice when it came, though cool to the point of absolute zero, sounded almost sweetly reasonable:

"It's your case, John."

He might have been saying: "If you wish to dive in a diving suit with a hole in it . . ."

"I know," said Brentford, and allowed it to be apparent that he was suffering.

"Ability to direct, to organise, to delegate and administer is what counts in the higher ranks, John."

Crawford seemed to think they were words of one syllable, suitable for the instruction of a recruit.

"You see, if you succeed," he said sweetly, and even with a smile, "what you'll have proved, John, is that you'd make a first-rate detective-sergeant."

"I know," said Brentford.

"While if you don't," Crawford said, "who knows? You might be liable to become one."

He got up and went for his hat.

CHAPTER NINETEEN

The breeze was stronger. The gentle sea-breeze, which had sprung up unnoticed on the estate in the morning, was filling in, and wavelets were sparkling on the rocks as they drove back to the creek from Loebeach.

"What did he say?" said Ball, interested.

They could see in all five policemen scattered around the creek, where the tide was full now, making the creek an arm of blue beneath the trees, with seagulls flighting overhead and waders round the shore. Two of the policemen were on the nearer bank, and one was on the far side, watching something from the Morris quay, and one was keeping back a knot or little crowd of spectators, some of whom had been there since the road was opened.

In answer, Brentford said: "Stop the car."

They drew up by the two policemen on the bank, with the spectators finding food for their curiosity by looking at the car. The younger of the two policemen, a constable, came up quickly when he saw them stop.

"What are you doing?" Brentford said.

The young man pointed it out to him, a log floating semi-submerged, mostly beneath the ripples of the lapping water. "Floating a log, sir. We put it in from the other side. It might be like the body. At this stage of the tide, it might show us where it would go."

"Whose idea was this?" said Brentford. He sounded short.

The older man, a sergeant, had come up to them by then.

"I take responsibility, sir," he said.

"I see. Just your own idea?"

"We were here. If you want—if you want to use us——" The sergeant reddened.

The experiment was useless, as Ball could see. With the breeze from seaward blowing gently in from the open creek-mouth, the wavelets had set up a surface drift. Already the log, in circumstances not at all like those of high tide in the stillness of the night, was following the course Morris had said his boat took when in a high wind it broke away. The log was steadily drifting up to the little bridge. What the experiment would prove was that the body could not have been where it had been.

"I am sorry, sir," the sergeant said, "if I have exceeded my authority."

"No, that's all right," Brentford said. "Carry on."

In fact, he was looking at the two rooftops that were visible through the trees on the farther bank. One, they now knew to be the Morris house. The other was farther down, where the creek made a bend to the river, and he did not know it. It was impossible that it could be the Silcrests' or Feltham's. A good position. It must be the Trueman-Davies'.

"Drive on," he told the driver. "We want to visit some other people. I believe their name is Trueman-Davies."

The driver re-started the car, and as they crossed the little bridge, Brentford spoke to Ball.

"The Super said I am a damn' fool," he said.

Ball grunted, but was too wise to express an opinion on that subject. He was sorry he had asked.

"It would be a relief if Crosston found that nightdress," he said. "Not that it proves anything if he does, but if he doesn't that doesn't even prove that it does not exist."

They were approaching the lodge-gate of the old estate, and Brentford said nothing.

"It's always a stroke of genius on the part of a desperate murderer, that," said Ball. "To invent, and stick to, some practical piece of evidence that the police have never found," He made conversation nicely.

They stopped at the gate though it was open. The old man was in the garden of his cottage and the driver asked him which branch of the drive to take to reach the Trueman-Davies'. Brentford wondered why he was back there, visibly.

"If you know which is Mr. Feltham's, don't go in there but keep on going," the old man said, looking at them without welcome as he leant on a garden rake.

It did not sound likely, but the driver nodded.

"A moment," said Brentford, and opened the car door.

"Who owns this estate?" he asked the old man.

The old man studied him and said: "All the gentlemen."

"What do they do?" said Brentford, "pay you wages or charge you rent?"

The old man looked sly and said: "I was here before they was; they can't shift me. They tried once, at the time they bought it."

" 'They?' "

"I told you. All the gentlemen."

Brentford returned his look for a moment, then closed the door. "Drive on," he told the driver.

They went up through the estate woods. Once they caught a glimpse of a line of police searchers among the trees.

Passing Feltham's, Brentford looked straight ahead. If Crosston was there and tried to wave to him or stop him, he did not see him. He watched the drive which continued at a higher level on the hillside above the woods, then plunged down through the woods again. The drive ran parallel with the creek and then descended. The Trueman-Davies' house was in the hollow of the hillside at the creek-mouth, and it was the one they had seen.

It was a long, low house, sheltered from the sea-winds but beautifully situated with a view both up the creek and down the creek across the bay. It was the only one of the houses on the estate that had the double view, and it was larger than the other houses, as though the architect had had the space and finance to spread himself. Below the house, the garden ran down towards the creek while a line of trees and shrubs gave privacy while permitting a patterned view of the blue of the water from the house itself.

"Wait," Brentford told the driver. He did not, this time, make the mistake of saying that his visit would only take five minutes, but he said, "Turn the car and be ready to leave," and he and Ball walked along the gravelled approach path to the verandah which was the major feature of the house.

Below them in the garden they could see a flash of colour, a woman down there in a summer dress. The house was not empty however, for a voice spoke to them from the verandah before they reached it.

"Are you the police?"

They went up the steps to the verandah and found Trueman-Davies, in a wheel-chair. They began to collect loose ends.

CHAPTER TWENTY

"Inspector Brentford and Sergeant Ball," Brentford said.

Trueman-Davies looked at them as though he had been expecting them but not as though, now they were here, he was pleased to see them, Ball noticed. He was a man no older than Feltham or Morris, but the blanket that was tucked around his knees, despite the weather, as he sat in the semi-mobile chair, ended above thin ankles and unmoving feet. No one had to tell them that he was a cripple.

"It's taken you long enough to get here," he said.

"Did you want to see us, Mr. Davies?"

"Trueman-Davies."

"Was there some particular reason for which you wished to see us, Mr. Trueman-Davies?"

"You don't think a man in my situation, with a daughter, might have a warning when there's a murder of the girl next door?"

Brentford turned and looked at the view from the verandah. It was all that he had expected. Across the garden and the trees, the creek led up to the right, while the curve of the bay and holiday beaches across the river were sufficiently distant to be chiefly effective, he imagined, as lines of lights at night. But the house was isolated. It was the kind of home that would only be chosen by a man who was both wealthy, and, seeking somewhere permanent, with little desire to participate or have social contacts with the world around him. Especially if that man were a cripple, and peculiarly if he had a youngish daughter.

"We were not aware you had a daughter, Mr. Trueman-Davies."

"Did you ask anyone?"

"No," Brentford admitted.

"Tessa!" Trueman-Davies called, turning to the house. "Tessa, come out here!"

Brentford indicated the direction of the creek while they were waiting: "You didn't happen to be looking out here at around, say, midnight last night?" he asked.

"No," said Trueman-Davies. "We were in bed. We hear of such things through tradesmen's vans."

Then the girl came out and she was of similar age to Caroline Silcrest.

But there the resemblance ended, Ball thought. The girl had dark, straight hair, a sallow skin, and a thin elongated body. She wore a brown dress and looked as though, before she had been called out, she had been curled up with a book in it.

"This is a police inspector, Tessa. Behave yourself, girl."

Ball wondered why it was necessary for him to say that.

He found out. The girl got as far as the door frame and leaned against it. She studied Ball and Brentford.

Then she said: "I suppose you know Daddy has a criminal record?"

Brentford, Ball saw, really looked at her.

"He has," she said.

"Tessa," said Trueman-Davies, more sad than anything else, Ball thought.

"Well, you were blamed when mother died!" She turned on him.

"That accident has nothing to do with this," said Trueman-Davies.

"Why don't you tell them?" she said. "Now they're here; that it wasn't justice?"

Trueman-Davies looked as though he might. He said regretfully: "The Inspector hasn't come about that."

He looked as though he still might. The girl left the door-frame and addressed Brentford:

"Why did you blame him for what he couldn't help?"

Brentford looked lost, and felt it, Ball thought.

"Even if he wanted to kill mother," Tessa said, "how could he possibly want to be made the way he is, for the rest of his life?"

She was knowingly indignant. At least she thought she knew, Ball thought. He watched Brentford make an effort.

"Your Father was right, Miss. It wasn't about this we came to see you."

Ball wondered if Brentford were sure about that. He looked as though he had enough to worry about already.

"Oh I know," she said scornfully. "We heard from the grocer's van."

"Let it alone, Tessa," Trueman-Davies said.

"I want to know," she said. That was the trouble, Ball thought, perhaps her father's trouble too. "Inspector, how can you charge a man with causing death and injury when he couldn't possibly have intended it?"

Brentford looked as though it were a riddle. He turned to Trueman-Davies.

"Sir——" he said.

"It's because I'm young," Tessa said. "It's because I'm young you're taking no notice of what I'm telling you."

Trueman-Davies made no attempt to stop her, Ball noticed. He seemed quite content that she should call him a wife murderer, if that was what she implied.

He just smiled sardonically at Brentford.

"Give the Inspector a chance, Miss," Ball said. He looked at Brentford for guidance. "We came about something else——?"

"If you ask her, she'll tell you about that too," Trueman-Davies said. "That girl has been asking to be murdered for a long time."

108

He looked at Tessa with affection.

Brentford too turned to her.

"If you know anything, Miss?" He swallowed, Ball saw. "You knew her as a neighbour?"

She looked at Brentford with pity.

"Father didn't let me have anything to do with her," she said with easy triumph. "I've seen her from the cliffs, if you want to know. Sunbathing naked with Dr. Feltham."

She looked at Brentford with interest.

"She's right," said Trueman-Davies. "You police should think. My evidence is you don't."

It sounded, Ball thought, like personal experience, as though he meant it.

It was becoming rather pointed that he had not asked them to sit down.

Tessa confirmed it: "You'll not get much out of Daddy, you know, after what you did to him."

That much was gratuitous information, but she had something personal too:

"I had to go to boarding school because of you."

A shadow fell across the verandah from behind them.

It was someone new, and, Ball hoped, relief.

"Henry, what are you thinking of?" the new voice said.

She looked young and beautiful, coming from the garden in her coloured dress, and it sounded far more hopeful.

"Are you the men from the police car? Won't you please sit down?"

She sounded young, bright and confident, a blonde.

CHAPTER TWENTY-ONE

"We seemed to be having some difficulty," Brentford admitted when they sat looking at the splendid view.

It was only the young, blonde, second Mrs. Trueman-Davies who looked concerned.

"Really, Henry——!" She looked chidingly at her husband.

Tessa would not accept that. "It's all very well for you, Penny," she said sullenly to her stepmother. "You weren't involved."

Penny spoke to her as a picture of sweet reason. "Any nurse is involved, Tessa. Quite apart from the fact I was marrying your father then."

"Yes," said Tessa. "That's how you were involved: that it let you marry him."

The blonde's voice was sharp, but without them present, Ball thought, it might be even sharper:

"Tessa, I won't have that kind of talk!"

Trueman-Davies surveyed his wife and daughter with some degree of satisfaction.

"What can we do for you?" he said to Brentford.

Brentford still looked helpless, but he said with some insistence: "When was all this, sir?"

Rather as though he had made up his mind he had to take it, Ball thought.

It was Penny Trueman-Davies who objected. Brightly and socially, she said: "Oh come, Inspector! Surely it wasn't about this you came to ask your questions?"

It hadn't been, Ball thought, until husband and daughter forced it down their throats.

"We are interested in the histories of the people on the estate," said Brentford cautiously.

"But all this happened a long time ago. It was only a car accident, you know!"

She seemed positively anxious for them to dismiss it, Ball thought, since it was only that.

"We like to know what people can tell us from their own knowledge," said Brentford.

"But if you let Henry——!"

"Perhaps if you tell us about yourselves first," said Brentford persuasively. "And then, after that, about the estate and the people on it?"

"I see." She sounded only half convinced.

"Inspector," Trueman-Davies said.

Brentford waited. Ball watched him wait.

"This was six years ago," Trueman-Davies said. "I had a thriving import business, of which I was the principal and buyer. I also had a wife and daughter. I was in love with my wife and loved my daughter. It was because I loved my wife that I was late driving to the plane one day."

Trueman-Davies did not tell Brentford why he was telling him all this.

"My wife was with me," he said. "I was driving, but she would drive the car back from the airport. We had an accident on the Great West Road. That was the accident in which my wife died. And for that you persecuted me."

The family tried to interrupt: "Pros——"

"I was paralysed and on my back in a plaster cast for six months. It was obvious, it would have been to a child, that I would neither drive nor walk again. But you police have different ideas. You prosecuted me on the charges of manslaughter and dangerous driving. It was my first contact with you and what you mean by road safety. I discovered that the word 'accident' has disappeared from your vocabulary. Your idea of road safety is to call someone a criminal and persecute him to the utmost rigour of the law. I imagined that even a policeman would see that I could not have intended to kill my wife and break my back, but I discovered I was wrong about policemen."

"We——" said Brentford, mildly.

"I even imagined I had been punished," Trueman-Davies said. "Being incapacitated, I had to sell my business, and my wife was dead. I was myself in pain and helpless. But road safety has nothing to do with that, it seems. I was summoned to court. I insisted on going there. I was carried in on a stretcher, to be scolded, fined. I was fined fifty pounds. You understand, fifty pounds? The accident, I should say, cost me ten thousand. My wife was dead. My daughter was motherless. People were still killing themselves on the Great West Road. But to stop it, with great intelligence, you fined me fifty pounds."

Ball was watching Brentford's expression. It interested him.

"Of course you didn't know what you were doing," Trueman-Davies said.

Brentford, Ball imagined, was trying to say something suitable. If so, he took too long.

"My daughter had gone to stay with my wife's parents," Trueman-Davies said. "They were full of sympathy until they heard the sentence of the court. Then they decided that the court had decided I had killed their daughter. I had to take Tessa away from them. They were beginning to talk to her about 'That terrible man, your father.' So there I was, in a nursing home, in a plaster cast, friendless and with a daughter with no one to look after her. You understand? You understand why I have a great affection for and belief in the wisdom of the police? I feel safer when you are there. Particularly when I travel about the roads. You know how we, the public, respect you, don't you? You appreciate why we say 'our police are wonderful', don't you?"

"I am not a traffic policeman," Brentford said.

"Henry——" said Penny Trueman-Davies.

"You see what you did to Daddy?" said Tessa Trueman-Davies fiercely. "And me and Grannie too——"

"About this matter of Caroline Silcrest——" Brentford said.

Looking at him, and though it was disrespectful, Ball thought he looked bewildered.

Or just discouraged.

Which he should not be.

CHAPTER TWENTY-TWO

A nursing home, Ball thought. A nurse.

"In time I'll come to the present," said Trueman-Davies grimly.

"Henry means this is how we married and came to the estate," Penny Trueman-Davies said.

"He hasn't got there yet," said Tessa.

"Nor is it necessary," the blonde said.

"Not that I don't appreciate your point of view, sir," Brentford said to Trueman-Davies.

"Do you?" said Trueman-Davies. "Do you actually want to hear about how I remarried and came here?"

"Well tell him if you must, Henry," Penny Trueman-Davies said. She turned to Brentford. "I am his nurse," she told him. "I was the one who took him into court on a stretcher. Naturally my sympathies were aroused." She looked momentarily coy, which did not suit her, and she seemed to know it. "We got on well, and that is all there is to tell."

"It isn't," said Tessa.

"Tessa never has become reconciled to her father's remarriage," Penny said seriously to Brentford.

"I see," said Brentford.

"Do you want me to tell you, or don't you?" said Trueman-Davies.

But he could not quite grip his family in the same way.

"Did you say which nursing home this was?" said Brentford.

"What do you want the name of the nursing-home for?" said Tessa.

"I am not likely to forget the Mary Cross Nursing Home," said Trueman-Davies.

"What did you say the name was?" Brentford asked.

"The Mary Cross," Penny said. "You've heard of it, Inspector?"

He might agree he had if they gave him time, Ball thought.

"It must have been quite an undertaking for a crippled man to come down here," Brentford said to Trueman-Davies.

"We heard of the estate, you see, from Mr. Feltham," Penny Trueman-Davies said with a nurse's air of mystery.

"I see," said Brentford. "You were Mr. Trueman-Davies' nurse, and Mr. Feltham was his doctor?"

"Don't be absurd, Inspector," Trueman-Davies said. "How could Feltham be my doctor?"

"Dr. Feltham is a gynaecologist, Inspector," Tessa said.

Penny Trueman-Davies spoke quickly, with the air of settling an argument before it started: "I heard about this estate from Mr. Feltham, Inspector, and I told Henry."

Ball looked quietly at Brentford.

"Was this before or after you decided to marry?" said Brentford.

"Well," said Penny, "it was about the same time. You know how it is, Inspector. Talking of marriage we had to think of where we were going to live."

"You might as well tell him the truth," said Trueman-Davies. "How we were going to live, since you were taking on a crippled man and his young daughter."

"What Daddy means is that this is what he offered her if she would marry him," said Tessa.

"Penny!"

"Well, you didn't take us on for nothing, did you?"

"That's quite enough of that, Tessa!"

Ball watched Trueman-Davies watching his wife and daughter squabble. He was surprisingly neutral, Ball saw. He would have thought he would have checked the daughter.

"Why shouldn't I say that?"

"Because it makes it look as though I married your father for his money!"

"Didn't you? Wasn't it that and——"

"Tessa," said Trueman-Davies.

Tessa blushed and looked angry and twisted in her chair, Ball saw. For a moment she looked as though she would go away.

"At least this estate was starting and being planned at the time we were being married," Trueman-Davies said to Brentford amicably.

"Would you tell me about that, sir?" Brentford said tentatively.

He had not shown any inclination to stop or interrupt the incipient quarrel between daughter and wife, Ball noticed; but Ball viewed the direct question to Trueman-Davies with apprehension, fearing another outburst.

Trueman-Davies was remarkably amenable, however. He seemed to have that fellow-feeling with Brentford for a moment that came between a man who had administered a castigation and the one who had suffered it.

"So far as I know it was like this," said Trueman-Davies.

"Feltham was approached by Silcrest, as an estate agent and patient of his, or rather the patient was his wife. He had acquired an option on this estate and he wanted one or two people to come in with him, to develop it for their own purposes, as a private venture. If you look at these houses, you'll see what he had in mind."

"And we heard about it from Mr. Feltham," Penny Trueman-Davies said.

Brentford showed an apparent inclination to disregard her, though perhaps not noticeably.

"It was advertised, sir?" he said to Trueman-Davies.

"Look at it, man! You don't advertise a thing like this. You cast about among your acquaintances."

Trueman-Davies showed signs of temper again and Brentford looked humble.

"So in fact you all knew one another before you came here?"

"If you can call it that. Silcrest knew Morris. They were business partners. A business acquaintanceship. At least Silcrest had some money invested in a factory that Morris ran at that time."

"So now you know all about us all, Inspector," Penny Trueman-Davies said.

Brentford turned to her mildly.

"Yes," he said calmly. "And now I can ask you the questions I came to ask you, such as where you all were last night." He sounded as though it just went on from there.

Ball watched with interest. He found it hard to guess why, but Penny Trueman-Davies, beautiful, young and self-assured as she was on her excellent verandah, in the midst of her family and before the gorgeous view, looked distinctly more taken aback than she should have been.

For a moment, Ball thought, she looked as though things worried her, not having gone quite according to her plan.

"Why, we were all here, Inspector!"

"All of you?" Brentford said with a deliberation that attracted attention, "And all the evening and all the night?" He sounded plainly curious.

"Inspector," Trueman-Davies said. "What is this? Don't be absurd!" He laughed softly.

"I am sorry, sir," said Brentford. "I have to know."

"You do know," said Trueman-Davies. "We were all here."

"Then did you have anyone else here with you, sir?"

Ball was jotting down the substance of the answers and not the detail. He found time to look at Penny.

He was right, she looked worried, he saw. And when Trueman-Davies said: "No one; we were alone," he thought: and well she might be.

Ball had a mind that was second to none, even Brentford's, for remembering who went in and out of a place, and who was where, and when.

"I went out for a walk," Penny Trueman-Davies said. "Don't you remember, Henry? Between nine and ten."

Brentford turned to her calmly and said: "You went for a walk at that time?"

She looked innocent now, Ball saw.

"Yes. I often do. I am free then, you see. Henry goes to bed around eight and I see him settled. Tessa," she looked at her stepdaughter with a shade of contempt, "is usually reading. So after I get Henry settled, I go out."

"Far?" said Brentford dryly.

"No. Of course not; how could I? I usually walk down through the woods to the sea and back, and that's where I went last night."

Brentford spoke deliberately: "Did you meet anyone last night, Mrs. Trueman-Davies?"

She looked him in the eye and said: "No."

Brentford was silent for a moment, Ball noticed, and so, he noticed with surprise, was everyone else.

It was just, Ball thought, as though they had run out of questions, and statements and counter-statements, or perhaps had outstayed their welcome.

If, that was, they had ever had one.

But Brentford smiled easily and said: "And so you were back by ten."

"About then," Penny Trueman-Davies said. She looked at her husband. "That was it, wasn't it Henry?"

"I don't know," said Trueman-Davies with an air of complete indifference. "I didn't look."

Which, Brentford appeared to indicate, concluded that.

He looked around him for a moment, admiring the view as though reluctant, and got up to go. Ball watched him with surprise.

After all, Ball saw, at that point they had two people, Helen and George Silcrest, out visiting the previous evening, who had not left the estate, it was said, and no one would acknowledge them. Not either, so far.

But Brentford did not appear to mind that. He smiled comfortably at the people on the verandah and said "Thank you for your assistance, Mr. and Mrs. Trueman-Davies, and you too, Tessa."

Then he led the way out, down the verandah steps, and to the car.

CHAPTER TWENTY-THREE

Ball was only partly familiar with Brentford's methods, and they puzzled him.

What you should do, Ball thought, was to find out exactly where everyone was, and when. If there were any discrepancies, you called on the people at once, or called them in for questioning, and ironed the details out. That was the police way, and as Ball knew, it worked.

Fifty per cent. of times, anyway. That was the percentage of crimes that were actually solved, Ball knew.

But Brentford moved slowly to the car and told the driver, whom Ball disapproved of, to drive slowly around the drive and away from the house, and when he was just getting out of sight of the house, at the curve of the woods, to stop there.

It was not that it was unorthodox, Ball thought, but that it was imbecilic.

Brentford got out of the car and looked down at the creek

and stretched his legs. He measured the angle of view to the house to see if they were in sight or not. Ball too got out. He said:

"You don't really imagine that the girl could have been brought all this way and put in the creek here, sir?"

It was, presumably, possible, if someone, laden with a body, could have scrambled through the bushes at the bottom of the slope below them, then climbed down a minor cliff.

Brentford showed himself on the drive and stood looking at the creek. He looked, Ball thought, as though he might send the driver down there. But when Penny Trueman-Davies came out of the house they had left, and moved down to resume her work in the garden, he came back to the car.

From there he watched the woman in the coloured dress move down to the bottom of the garden, along by the creek, and then come up to them.

It was that people would actually do it, Ball thought, that took a little understanding.

"I am glad you are still here, Inspector." She was a little out of breath.

Brentford offered her a seat in the car, but she stood looking occasionally back anxiously at the house as though to be sure she could not be seen from it.

"It would have been easy enough for you to make an excuse to go shopping and call at the police station tomorrow," he said mildly. "It was only to save my time and yours that I thought you might like to talk to me today."

"You do understand why I had to lie to you with my husband there? A man in his position. Naturally, he's senstive and inclined to jealousy. Like most invalids, he's inclined to imagine things!"

"I can understand it must be awkward for you, Mrs. Trueman-Davies," Brentford said with a glance that surveyed the young bright woman.

"If he had known I met George Silcrest when I went out last night, he would think I did it every time. I wouldn't be able to stir from the house at all!"

"You don't meet him every time then, when you go out for an evening walk?"

118

"Inspector, are you implying something?"

"It would help me to establish Mr. Silcrest's actions better if I knew whether he met you by accident or as a regular thing, by prearrangement."

"You can't be very interested in the father of a murdered girl, Inspector. What you really mean is that you will know me better if you know whether I am in the habit of meeting George Silcrest each evening after I have done my nurse's duty and put my husband into his bed."

"You regard yourself as his nurse?" Brentford saw she was about to reply sharply. "Let me explain," he said. "I don't have to tell you in detail why I ask my questions, Mrs. Trueman-Davies, but there are considerations you may not have thought of. Caroline herself, for instance. I have to establish if she knew where her parents were, and at what time she could expect them back."

She stood looking at him frowning for a moment. It was not difficult for Ball to guess that she was realising that that was a question he would also ask George Silcrest, and that the parents, as happened in such circumstances, would have an interest in saying that of course the children knew where they were and would have no difficulty in calling them in case of trouble.

"I think you will understand the kind of arrangement I made with Henry, in the nature of things, Inspector."

"What kind of an arrangement did you make?"

"He was both a sick and desperate man. He didn't exaggerate his position or loneliness in the nursing home. He was wealthy, of course, but people exaggerate the kind of thing that can be done with money, unless it really is unlimited. He wanted to set up a new home for Tessa. Also he needed a competent nurse to look after him. I was really sorry for him. He would have needed a large house, to accommodate a housekeeper and a nurse, and also a staff of servants to look after the four of them. Nobody can do those things these days unless they are at least a millionaire. I agreed to marry him. But naturally I expected a certain degree of freedom in return. I didn't contract or promise him to see him and his daughter and no one else."

"So you are suggesting that your husband can't really complain if you have been seeing George Silcrest regularly in the evenings?"

"Complain, certainly not! But that is another matter from drawing it to his attention. As his nurse with a sense of responsibility, as well as his wife for convenience, I would not openly point out to him facts that might excite him."

She looked challengingly at Brentford, asking him if he was going to be rash enough to try to tell her how she should rule her own conscience over the conflicting duties of wife and nurse to a sick man.

Brentford seemed to think about it. "It must have been quite an undertaking and decision for you too," he said. "Knowing you were going to get into this kind of position if you married him."

He turned a little, looking past her at the grounds of her beautiful house, with its view of creek and woods, and it was not impossible for her to interpret his statement, if she chose, as a question about how she had come to do it, and whether she had found it worth it.

She did not hesitate to answer, and her tone was one of calm simplicity: "The position of a private nurse always is a difficult one, Inspector. There is no other profession where at one moment you may be regarded as a paid servant and the next find yourself firmly giving orders and expecting unquestioning obedience from everyone in the house. That was the prospect before me when I was fully qualified, as I was when I met Henry and was thinking of taking up private practice. And one thing I had decided was that I would either marry him first, before we came here, or never marry him and act only as his nurse. Nurses who start out as the nurses of terminal cases and then marry their wealthy employers just before they die are naturally regarded with suspicion. In his case too, there was not only his wealth but also the complication of his daughter. I chose to let people say I took advantage of him if they liked, but to get it crystal clear before I started."

"I see," said Brentford. He did see presumably: that the young woman was very sure of herself and was putting a bold face on it. Many would have rejected all questions with indignation and insisted that they had married Henry Trueman-Davies for love alone.

Her way of telling it was at least more credible, Ball thought. A nurse was perhaps the last person on earth to regard a wealthy fractious invalid as a romantic figure, and she was not even denying that she had secured herself a position from which she could not be dismissed, with the prospect of a very considerable inheritance, despite the daughter, when, as she hinted was liable to happen, her patient died. Brentford continued speaking.

"Thank you for coming to see me and being frank, Mrs. Trueman-Davies," he said. "I am taking it that you have been seeing Mr. Silcrest regularly, and that your movements were forecastable, and quite the usual thing."

She nodded with an expression of slight distaste, as though she still did not like it put quite like that, but said: "Is there anything else you want to ask me?"

"Not at present, but there are always afterthoughts. It's quite possible that I will need to see you later."

"If you do, use the telephone and I will make an excuse to go shopping and will call on you at the police station as you suggest."

"Thank you," he said.

"Not at all. I hope you catch this terrible man and relieve us of the anxiety we naturally feel for Tessa while he's still at large." She sounded insincere.

She turned and walked away, back the way she had come, towards the garden.

Brentford turned the other way and looked up and down the hillside, and particularly at the woods. He was slow in his movements and seemed even a little reluctant as Ball led him impatiently towards the car.

He need not have worried however. They had got into the car and driven only a little way along the drive before, emerging from the bushes, the brown-dressed, dark, untidy and not altogether attractive figure of Tessa was waving them to stop.

And Feltham had only incidentally mentioned the nurse, Ball thought.

CHAPTER TWENTY-FOUR

Brentford was more open-minded about it, despite a certain
anxiety that possessed him. Some more, he thought.

Tessa stood in the drive in front of their approaching car
with one hand raised. She looked as though she were not too
sure they would stop, and was ready to jump aside into the
bushes. It was odd, Brentford thought. For the Trequayne
estate. She looked as though life had always treated her like
that: like something that was oncoming, bigger than she was,
and from which, at any moment, she might have to save
herself.

Yet when they did stop, and he opened the car door, she
took a little time coming to them. She stood near the bonnet of
the car, looking back the way they had come, and only reluctantly came to him when he spoke to her.

"What is it, Tessa?"

"Has she been speaking to you?" she said.

She spoke of her stepmother as though to say: "Have you
been treating with the enemy?" If they had, it was useless for
her to speak to them, she seemed to imply.

Brentford nodded. She had almost certainly seen the conversation. Tessa stood a few feet from the car, looking vaguely
towards the house.

"I suppose you know she lied to you?" she said.

They had wondered not if, but why, since concealment of a
love-life seemed not habitual on Trequayne.

Brentford wondered whether to get out to her.

"You would have to know what she said just now, to know
that, wouldn't you, Miss?" he said.

She looked as though she would flee to the woods if he
approached. But the formal "Miss" seemed to sting her.

She turned round on him with her lips parted. And she was
surprisingly aware of their preoccupations, derived from
Feltham's story.

"She didn't hear of this estate from Dr. Feltham! She and

George Silcrest were lovers before she ever met Daddy! It was all a plot to use Daddy and his money to get her here!"

Her voice was defiant and she looked as though she might be about to weep at any moment.

Brentford watched her. This was too quick, he thought.

He had had enough indications that what the stepdaughter alleged might be the case. "The nurse" of Feltham's story, who had destroyed the Silcrest marriage, was hardly likely to be another. It was only that he had been reluctant to believe it. His impressions of Penny had been that she was lying, but without proof he had not been prepared to believe that the matter was as simple, or the young woman as bad, as that, or that it was even relevant. Especially the last.

"How do you know this, Tessa?" he asked her.

"What does it matter how I know it? Why do you believe her? Do you think it even could be true, that she, a young nurse, should hear it from a big consultant surgeon? That's only what she told Daddy!" She did weep.

She was referring to Penny's account of how Trueman-Davies had been introduced to the estate. He thought back to the conversation on the verandah.

"Your father didn't deny it," he said.

She looked desperate.

Brentford got out of the car.

"How was Daddy to know that she only planned to marry him so that she could come here too when George Silcrest did? Someone who looks like her? How could he know?"

She looked away from Brentford as she spoke, as though seeking which way to jump in case he, outraged by her words, as she apparently thought he might be, tried to seize her.

Brentford was careful to make no unexpected move. He believed it was more important that he should keep still than that he should attend her with politeness.

"You seem to suggest your father is something of a fool, Tessa."

She stared at him, looking shocked.

"If, after living here all this time, he still doesn't suspect," he said.

She looked unbelieving.

"But he does! He knows! That's what's awful. He keeps her here to keep a home for me, and he lets her say what she likes in case I should get to know, and I daren't tell him I do know, and she takes advantage of both of us and everyone."

She looked at Brentford as though he could untie the Gordian knot into which the family had tied itself.

"Why are you telling me this, Tessa?"

She looked back up the hillside of bushes and trees through which she had made her circuitous route from the house. For a moment he thought that she was going to go that way, to depart as quickly as she had arrived. But she thought better of it, turning back to him and stepping back a little, more nervously than before.

"She killed Caroline Silcrest," she said. Then she looked at him as though she expected to be beaten for such a statement.

Brentford said nothing. Tessa eyed him wildly, then looked to see, hopefully, if it was possible he believed her.

"There's the other one, you know!" she said. "She'll murder him next!"

Brentford looked around to see if there was a tree-trunk to sit on. There was not, so that he had to make do as they were.

"Which other one?" he asked in a tone that was sensible and practical and not too pressing.

"Caroline's brother! The other reason she and George Silcrest can't go off together!"

Brentford pursed his lips and stood in an attitude of thought. He visibly, to Tessa at least, followed the logic of the operation.

"Wouldn't she need some money to do that?" he asked. "Wouldn't she very likely murder you and your father too?"

Expressions chased one another across Tessa's face. She believed that Brentford was laughing at her, and then she believed that he believed her, and then she doubted.

"You know, Tessa," Brentford said quietly. "This kind of thing either is so, or it isn't." He was grave.

She did as he expected. She looked as though she were very

nearly ready to weep again. Only it was not with rage, but with helplessness, frustration.

There was only one place he could take her, and that was into the car. He jerked his head at Ball, who got out of the back seat and into the front with the driver. Brentford put his hand on Tessa's arm and took her into the back.

She sat looking dry-eyed out at the woods which she must know so well.

"There must be some reason why you say these things, Tessa," he said in his quiet tone.

She turned and looked at him, and seemed to see him for the first time. He was not an abstraction, a policeman, or something to be invoked, the majesty of the law, but a solid man who was prepared, unexpectedly, to listen to her, to what she had to say.

"You don't know how it is when you are growing up," she said.

Brentford said nothing. He doubted if she would realise that he had grown up in quite a similar way.

She looked out at the woods again. "I didn't realise," she said. "Or only in a way. Daddy's getting married again and our coming here had been romantic. You wouldn't know. And then I was away at school. It was difficult for me to realise that things weren't what they seemed. I suppose I expected Daddy and Penny to be—like Daddy and Mummy had been. But they weren't."

He felt her shiver on the seat beside him.

"I don't know what made me slip out of bed and follow her one night," she said.

Brentford believed she did. She was still her father's daughter. She would not lack spirit.

He began cautiously to think ahead. He was in difficulties. He should transfer her to a policewoman to hear that story. But they might never hear the story if he made a move. He wisely remained silent and did nothing.

"It seemed so impossible," she said, "out there in the night among the trees. I wanted to run back and tell Daddy, as though he could stop it. I don't think I'd realised till then what Daddy had become. Besides, I couldn't believe it. I hadn't

125

known that grown-up people could behave like that. I wanted to go away, but I couldn't. I could only crawl nearer, to listen to what they said."

She laughed shakily, with a pseudo-sophistication that, from her actions, she could not sustain. From the standpoint of an uncertain sixteen years, which were not even a confident sixteen, she was looking back at a time when she was presumably fourteen or fifteen as though across a gulf.

"They were quarrelling. In a way. That was what I couldn't understand. I mean the way she was with Daddy, and that she should meet someone else, and love him and at the same time quarrel. I couldn't understand what they said. Not that night. I can't even remember if it was that night or another night I followed her. He said: 'I told you I'd never leave Helen and the children. She'd get custody in any court.' He was talking about divorce! I don't think I even understood what the words meant. But he said distinctly: 'I told you that before we came here.'"

She looked at Brentford as though he should understand a whole world from those two phrases, and perhaps he did.

But he could hardly be expected to be as shocked as she was. He had, after all, heard Feltham.

"It's not a lot, is it, Tessa?" he asked her carefully.

She stared at him. "Don't you realise? They had talked about it before they ever came here. That meant she had been with him before she ever married Daddy! And that meant— don't you see?—they *used* Daddy. He used his money to make his estate and she used him to get him to marry her and bring her here. And poor Daddy—if he even knew or realised since, what could he do about it?" Her eyes filled with tears and she looked at Brentford as though she expected him to go at once and arrest her stepmother and George Silcrest.

Brentford found his position difficult: "Even if this is true, Tessa——"

"Of course it's true! Do you think I haven't thought of it? Do you think I didn't think carefully before I came to you?"

"Even if it's true, it's hardly a thing about which you can invoke the law."

He thought her glance was that of a young girl looking at a fallen idol, and then he saw it wasn't. It was not impotence she was accusing him of, but stupidity.

"Don't you see how that shows she murdered poor Caroline, and how, what you said but didn't believe, she might murder me and poor Daddy next?"

"No I don't, Tessa."

She could hardly believe he could be so stupid. It took her a moment to realise it, and then she began to spell it out for him in simple words.

"It's what Penny is like! Don't you understand? To marry a sick man like Daddy when she already had a lover. And not only to marry him, but to use him to take her to where she could be with her lover. To live a lie like this. What kind of a woman could do that? And what was he like, George Silcrest, to let her do it? Just because he needed money for the estate. Think of his poor wife! But it was planned! It was a conspiracy, a plot! And why should a woman who would do that stop at anything? What kind of a love has she got for George Silcrest, to make her do a thing like this? She must be mad about him, and prepared to do anything. But it wasn't like she thought it was. Perhaps she thought his wife would leave him when she saw what he had done to her, bringing his lover to live as another man's wife nearby. But Helen didn't. And Penny was still dissatisfied. Doesn't the fact they were quarrelling show that? What Penny really wanted was him. I heard her say: 'I love you,' and he said, 'Penny, I won't desert the children.' So what could she do? It was poor Caroline and her brother who stood in her way, and if she murdered Caroline and made it look as though a man had done it—she's clever—clever!"

Brentford looked at the back of Ball's neck as he sat in the front seat writing inconspicuously.

Writing, he wondered, to what purpose?

He met her eyes again: "Tessa, you don't really believe this, do you?"

She began to cry, "It's true; it's true!" and Ball turned to look at him, surprised that he should challenge her whether it were true or not.

"It's easy to imagine these things," Brentford told her.

She looked at him with hatred, with the same helpless, dismayed look he had seen her use on her stepmother. Then she moved from him. Before he could have stopped her, had he tried, she squirmed out of the car again, through the open door, and went running up the hillside.

They sat in the car watching her.

"She's some girl, that," the driver said.

Ball was looking at Brentford. It was not for him to criticise his Chief Inspector, but he was frankly puzzled, and he ventured to say it.

"Why, sir? Even if we don't believe—couldn't we have pretended to believe and told her her allegations would be investigated in the proper way?"

If it was not criticism, it was as near as a sergeant could come with a chief inspector.

Brentford watched Tessa Trueman-Davies as she ran up the hillside and circled behind the bushes that would hide her from the house as she made her way back to it along the ridge.

"I didn't say I didn't believe her," he said mildly. "It's she who didn't believe. Or didn't realise what it was that she was saying."

They still sat on in the car, in the sunlit woods, and Ball and the driver waited for Brentford while he looked out, not apparently looking at anything in particular, but at the woods themselves.

He tried to express it, the consideration that, from the time in the Morris house that morning, had given him a preoccupation with the estate.

"How much intrigue, love, and connection between the people do you usually get in a place like this?"

The driver was turning on the radio, which he had turned off when Tessa came to the car, and it was the loudspeaker that seemed to answer him.

"Quantitatively?" Brentford said.

The girl's voice sounded pleasant on the summer air:

"...King thirteen. Peter King thirteen. This is your third call. I have a message for you."

They listened. Brentford slammed the car door and motioned to the driver, who put the car in motion.

Something was happening on the estate.

Brentford looked as though he had almost forgotten that events could happen, as well as talk.

CHAPTER TWENTY-FIVE

Inspector Crosston, the loudspeaker told them, had a report for Chief Inspector Brentford.

They went in search of Crosston, with two hundred yards to go to where they had left him. That did not mean he was still there.

A uniformed constable was, however, when they came to the junction of Feltham's drive. He signalled them to stop, much as Tessa had done, but looked more likely to die in the attempt.

He came to the car window with news of great import: "They've found it, sir!"

The constable was looking into the woods with shining eyes, sideways from the car.

Brentford sat still for a moment, and Ball watched him. So this was it, Ball thought.

The Superintendent had said that Brentford was wasting his time on the estate. Love affairs, personal involvements and human feelings were all very well, but only one time in a million was a murder the outcome.

The nightdress would show. If the nightdress had been found (and it was something that there even was a nightdress), then that meant presumably, probably, the scene of the crime. There was usually some evidence at the scene of the crime.

Brentford got out of the car.

"Where?" he asked the Constable.

"This way, sir. The Inspector said I was to wait and bring you, sir."

He started off into the woods, bulldozing his way through the bushes at the side of the drive. He went at an angle to the drive, but in the direction of the Silcrest and Morris houses.

They followed him in single file. And that was something, Brentford thought. In daylight it was difficult enough to keep their position clear when they went at right angles to the circuitous drive. At night, a stranger would hardly have found his way. If it was a place a stranger could hardly find, it pointed to a resident of the estate.

"There's a kind of footpath, sir," the Constable said. But he himself did not seem too sure of his direction. They were heading for the deeper woods, and the slanting sunlight on the upper branches made all the trees alike. He had to veer from his course to find the path.

There was no doubt, however, when they came near it.

It looked like a public meeting: a political demonstration, or a woodland meeting of some strange sect. They saw one man walking among the trees, and then another. Then they came to a circle of searching men. In the centre, around a cleared space, there was a thicker crowd of men called in from the general search.

Crosston and, oddly, Feltham, seemed to be the celebrants of the rite. They were surprised to see Feltham.

"Keep back——!" Crosston said, turning to where the crowd had split for them, until he saw who Brentford and Ball were. "Keep your feet off the ground," he told the Constable, changing his scowl to him.

Feltham, looking pale, and with his gaze fixed on a clump of briars in a gap in the trees, had not even turned.

"It's it," he said to Brentford.

He looked like a man who had had a hard time of it, both that morning and now again. They had left him with Crosston.

Crosston looked from him to Brentford. He took notice of where Brentford and Ball were walking, on the ground where evidence might lie. He moved his head towards Feltham. "I sent for him to come and identify it where it was," he told Brentford. He did not sound kind.

Ball and Brentford could see it now. It was a pale and

slightly tattered looking scrap of silk hung up on the briars beside the trodden path or foot-track.

It looked as though it had been thrown or hung there, Brentford thought, standing still, not on the path, and looking at it. And that was wrong. It should have been hidden. They had all imagined that. Or taken away.

Crosston went to Feltham, who was still staring fascinated at the nightdress that he had last seen, according to his story, with the live girl inside it. "You're sure?" he asked.

Feltham looked unwillingly at Crosston. He had reached that stage of unwillingness reached by witnesses who had already said so much that they could not remember exactly what they had said. But he confirmed the identification.

"Unless there are two nightdresses like that round the estate. Do you think that likely?"

To say that Feltham was unwilling, and fascinated, did not mean he had lost his self-possession.

"It's the right colour, size and shape?"

"It's the right colour. If you want me to identify the size, man, you'll have to pick it up."

Brentford was turning slowly and looking at the little clearing or gap in the trees. Two men, one of them a sergeant, were already working in detail along the path, examining all the footprints. There was material ready for taking plaster casts. So far as Brentford could see nothing had been forgotten.

But Feltham had seen Brentford and was looking at him now.

"They're wasting their time!" he said. "Anyone on the estate might have come this way on their way to bathe."

Feltham evidently felt his position of "helping the police in their inquiries". He made it more than that. He was more recovered from the morning than he looked, and he took it on himself to advise the police, which was a little different. "Caroline in particular would come this way," he said, "wearing her shoes or sandals——!" he stopped, and was struck by something: "Where are her shoes?"

Brentford looked at Crosston, and they had a sinking feeling when Crosston shook his head.

"We haven't found them yet," he said, and glanced at the

men who were searching in concentric circles. It was obvious what they were doing.

"Where are her sandals?" Feltham said. "She was wearing a pair of sandals."

Crosston turned on him.

"You're sure of that?"

Feltham looked at the Sergeant who was examining the path. "Have you found any barefoot imprints there?" he asked. He used a sarcastic voice.

The Sergeant looked up at Crosston. Crosston looked at Feltham then back at the Sergeant. "Well, have you?" he asked. Inexplicably, the Sergeant was looking dubious.

The Sergeant stood up and pointed to places he had marked with twigs.

"There are foot prints of a girl in light soles," he said. "There, there and there."

"Old ones or new ones?"

"We haven't found any print over one of them yet."

"Well, what is it man?"

The Sergeant looked as though he did not know how to say it.

"They go on," he said.

"They go on?"

"Past the nightdress!" the Sergeant said. He pointed. "She may have stopped. But they go on! As though she went on walking after she lost the nightdress . . ." He looked away.

Brentford stood looking at the ground. The scene of the crime, he thought.

"Just her footprints," he heard the Sergeant saying. "Going and coming. The only recent ones."

It would be like that, Brentford thought. In a place where the ground was soft under the trees. Where footprints would last, where it would even be possible to see where there had been a struggle, with pollen and grass stains that would cling to a suspect's clothes. He felt it was unjust. He listened to Crosston.

"Damn it, man; she can't just have taken off the nightdress and walked on without it! To walk through the woods in a thing like that is bad enough——"

"I don't know, sir." The Sergeant's face had gone wooden.

"What do you make of that?" Crosston asked Brentford, and Brentford did not answer.

Feltham, looking at a police force at a loss with a slight smile that, despite his pallor, carried an element of triumph or satisfaction, said: "Perhaps she did." He had a knowing air.

Even before then, somehow, inexplicably, they had all been looking at Feltham. Only now they were disbelieving.

Perhaps it was the sense that, when it came to answers in the case, Feltham was the only one who knew.

He looked at them as though he did know, and, knowing, could not resist it. "She took it off," he said. "You don't know Caroline." He sounded quite sure.

Brentford had turned and watched him silently. Feltham did not like his gaze and reacted quickly.

He went to the nightdress, where it hung, all too conspicuously, as they had all seen, on the briars. He touched it, then lifted the hem, showing them, the police, the results of his observation:

"Torn! You see? Have you seen a girl walk in one of these, with it floating out behind her——?"

"Don't guess, Feltham."

"I don't guess! She had to take it off, or lose it piece by piece as it caught on snags——"

"And she walked through the woods stark naked?" Crosston said.

"What else?" said Feltham. "Except for her shoes, that you haven't found."

"I don't believe it." Crosston said. "I'm damned if I do!"

Which, Brentford thought, looking at Feltham and his expression saying it, did not make any difference to the case or to what Feltham said.

It was a case in which, if Feltham's guess were true, and it seemed in accordance with what Feltham had been saying all along, the victim had sought her own demise. There was little else, it seemed, to be deduced from the silent woods.

And Feltham rubbed it in.

"Poor Caroline." He had moved away from the nightdress and was addressing them in a kind of declaration. "It's the kind of thing she would do. So reckless! To walk naked in the woods at midnight! And what are you doing, you police? Questioning us here? We wouldn't have touched Caroline. You haven't grasped it."

He turned, looked at them with his lips twisting, and began to go away, presumably back home.

"Mr. Feltham," Brentford said before he had taken more than a step or two towards the woods.

Crosston was looking at Feltham as though he would like to arrest him, Crosston had brought Feltham to the nightdress, and there had been something in Crosston's mind, Brentford saw. The hope that the suspect, Feltham, confronted by the nightdress where he himself had put it, would break down, confess. Crosston too believed in the estate.

It had not happened that way. But Feltham, hearing Brentford's call, looked shaken as he turned to look at him.

"We'll come back with you," Brentford said. "Our car's in that direction. We'll come back with you towards the house."

Feltham did not look happy about the prospect, but Brentford, closing with him, and with Ball following behind, leaving Crosston and his men to go on searching, said: "We'll have another little talk."

With Feltham? Ball thought. Brentford must be desperate now.

CHAPTER TWENTY-SIX

We have talked enough with Feltham, Ball thought, walking back with him and with Brentford, through the woods.

It was not, he thought, that Feltham did not have more to say, but would he say it? He looked at the shadows of the trees. The afternoon was almost over. They had had lunch late, and had spent a fair amount of time, too much time if Brentford did not believe Tessa at the Trueman-Davies. Brentford's day, the day he was giving to the swift following of the immediate evidence in the case, was running out. As was inevitable, if Feltham's contention was right.

He listened to him talking to Brentford. Feltham was talking, always talking. And the fact that he was saying no more than had already occurred to such minds as Superintendent Crawford could not make it easier for Brentford to bear.

"Caroline would sunbathe naked on the beach," Feltham said. "I didn't object. I doubt if anyone on the estate objected, except her parents. She was that kind of girl. I think I told you. But she wouldn't—she wouldn't have the same feeling about taking off that nightdress and going through the woods without it that another girl would."

Which led to the conclusion, the obvious conclusion of her meeting with a chance intruder.

Brentford was patient. His tone was patient. But Ball was surprised he did not talk about what Feltham said.

"You saw her walk away from your home last night?"

Feltham too was mildly surprised. "I told you that."

"Yes," said Brentford calmly. "And I believed you. You know these paths quite well? Does it surprise you I believed your story about how she left you? It sounded convincing. It had the ring of truth."

Feltham looked suspicious for a moment, and then relieved. He drew himself up a little as they walked. After a moment he said, "Thank you." By then, he made it sound as though it were no more than he had a right to expect.

"But you knew she was going home," Brentford said quite calmly in the same tone as before.

Feltham looked suspicious again and flashed a wary glance at him.

"You knew which path she would take." Brentford said. "It would be easy, wouldn't it? You know these paths. You only had to get out your car, drive round the drives, and come in at the far end of the path to head her off."

Feltham stopped walking. He stood stock still in the woods. He looked at Brentford and then around him. Except for Ball, there was no one else in sight.

"Is this an allegation, Inspector? This is what you think? It is what you were thinking when you said that you believed me?" His nervous face accused Brentford of treachery. He suddenly looked excited.

Brentford had stopped with him. Looking at him seriously, he said: "I want to know."

"Then no! I tell you no! It was not like that!"

Instead of accepting the statement, Brentford said quietly: "It would seem a reasonable thing for you to do."

"Reasonable?"

"To murder her."

Feltham stood looking at him with his face working. He was shocked by what had been sprung on him. And yet he made the effort.

"Reasonable? For me to murder her? Think what you are saying, Inspector! Why? Why should I murder her? You tell me that. The girl had offered herself to me. Poor Caroline! I, if anyone, I had no cause to kill her. You remember what I told you? Poor Caroline was the girl who had accused me and other men of trying to rape her. Who would have believed her if she had said the same again? Even if it were true? I had no cause to murder her!"

"The same argument seems to apply to everyone."

"Everyone, yes, except a stranger who did not know that by her foolishness she had made herself defenceless." Feltham was sharp and triumphant. "I told you! She took off that nightdress. She was wandering naked in the woods, and then——!" Feltham dropped his voice. "Poor Caroline," he said. But it did not seem to be Caroline he was thinking of.

Brentford watched him, not hurrying, remaining with him standing by the pathside in the woods.

"Unless by any chance you had got her pregnant," he said. He looked at Feltham calmly.

Feltham looked startled, then shook his head.

"Not Caroline." He looked worried however. "You mean—— You have news that she——?" His face looked anguished.

"We haven't got the doctor's report as yet."

Brentford watched Feltham closely as he looked relieved. But then he would, he thought. It would not necessarily have been Feltham who had got the girl pregnant.

"And then, Mr. Feltham," he said almost idly, "the other thing." He held Feltham motionless in the woods.

Feltham stared. He was highly wary now, and frightened.

Brentford said seriously: "Girls aren't murdered only because they have been slept with, Mr. Feltham. Not even because they won't. Sometimes it's because they will."

Feltham frowned, looked puzzled, slightly wild.

"Have you ever heard of Jack the Ripper and similar cases?" Brentford's voice was calm.

Whether Feltham had or not, he said: "Inspector, don't be absurd!" He hit a high-pitched tone.

Brentford showed no signs of feeling he was absurd.

The whole thing was odd, Ball thought.

"Supposing all the story you told me is true. Even to the point that you did not—that no intimacy took place between you and Caroline Silcrest." Brentford spoke quite calmly.

Feltham looked at him with a cautious, wary stupefaction.

"You saw her leaving," Brentford said, returning to the point from which he started. "You stood at your door, I think you told us. You saw her going off into the woods in the night. In the light from the door, I should guess. And the moonlight. A girl in a nightdress." Brentford looked at the woods around them, drew Feltham's attention to them. "And she had offered herself to you, and you had refused her. And what did you feel then?"

"I told you! Anger. Disappointment. I felt a little sick——" Feltham spoke with great rapidity.

"Anger?" said Brentford. His tone was quiet. "I wonder why that was? Because she had tempted you? Because she had tempted you and you had lost your chance? Because she knew you better than you did, and if she had kept on a moment longer you would have fallen?"

"No! I tell you no!" Feltham's tone was surprisingly heated in the quiet woods. It was almost a scream, Ball thought.

"It does happen like that," said Brentford mildly.

He watched Feltham's mouth working, making words that brought no sounds. His voice grew in weight a little.

"A moral man," said Brentford. "You are a moral man, Feltham? Or a careful one? They feel like that. That there are

137

some temptations that are beyond all bearing. Especially if they have not realised it before, just why they have been fascinated by the temptress. Such people, I am told, you perhaps feel a raging fury. Because they have been tempted. Because they have nearly fallen. Because, although they never expected it, if they don't do something drastic they are about to fall. And the fury has an object. A moral object."

It was surprising how calm Brentford's voice was, Ball thought, despite its weight.

"No!" cried Feltham. "This is outrageous! I tell you no!" He looked likely to be sick at any moment.

"After all, it's the girl who does the tempting, isn't it?" said Brentford. "Or is it? At least, there would be no temptation if there were no girl. And so what would have been more natural than for you to get the car out, drive round—that would be easy—and meet, head off, and 'remove' the girl? You're a natural murderer, Feltham. Except in one condition, you had to be."

Feltham went pale.

He stood quite still in the woods, and it astounded Ball that he did not ask what that condition was.

Yet he seemed at that point to recover his dangerously slipping self-control.

"Inspector," he said, and licked his dry lips. "Can I go home?"

Brentford waited a while before he answered him, Ball noticed, watching Feltham and appearing to assess him.

Then: "Yes, Mr. Feltham, you can go," he said.

They watched Feltham walking off, seeming to stagger slightly, before they turned and went slightly in the other direction towards the car.

Ball looked puzzled. Once or twice as they went back to the car he came up alongside Brentford and looked at him.

He expected Brentford to say something, but Brentford did not.

CHAPTER TWENTY-SEVEN

Poor Brentford, Ball thought. They were sitting in the car, and the driver, from the front seat, was turning round and waiting for his orders. Brentford was looking at the afternoon shadows of the trees across the drive. They were even longer now.

Ball was a dutiful and loyal man. He liked to feel with the detective-inspector or chief-inspector with whom he was working on a case. If possible, he liked to share his mind. It was not usually so easy. Normally the inspector would be in his office, or visiting the scene of the crime at intervals as Crawford did. Men like Ball got statements from witnesses or informants and took them in. Often the first a sergeant knew that there was something in the wind was when he received orders to go and visit a certain person and bring them in. Or the inspector would appear suddenly, give orders to assemble a force, and be on the spot when they surrounded a certain house. It should be easier than that with Brentford.

"I don't know that the evidence of that nightdress is conclusive," said Ball. "On the face of it, Feltham's explanation is a tall one. Wandering naked in the woods. I don't believe it."

Brentford went on looking along the drive. He said: "I think I do."

Which was not a good reply to an attempt at comfort, Ball thought. Brentford had told Ball after lunch that Crawford had thought him a bloody fool. Presumably for sticking to the estate instead of scouring the countryside. And if the girl had been wandering naked in the woods, and Feltham, for some inexplicable reason, had been sent home, dismissed, and Tessa Trueman-Davies was not believed, it looked to Ball even more likely that Crawford was right.

Brentford was proverbially up a gum tree.

Ball put his mind to it. Brentford had decided that someone, somewhere, on the Trequayne estate, had something to do with Caroline Silcrest's murder. Never mind why. He had.

And that being so, unless it turned out that way, Brentford was going to be an uncomfortable man to live with.

At least there ought to be some way of making it look as though someone on the estate were at least involved.

"There's William Morris," Ball said. "I know it means going back to where we started, but he didn't tell us where he was last night."

Brentford said impatiently: "We know. He was with Helen Silcrest."

He did not even want any help or comfort, it seemed to Ball. He just went on thinking for about three minutes, looking out at the drive, at the Trequanye woods, and appearing nervously involved, not exactly as he did when talking to a suspect.

Which being so, Ball thought, the only thing to do was to let him fry.

"Betty Keen," Brentford said, as though his process of ratiocination had led him to that name.

Ball simply looked at him. In all his searching for a possible murderer among the denizens of the Trequayne estate, the last name Ball would have come up with was that of Betty Keen.

"William Morris's common-law wife," said Brentford. He gave the driver his orders, which the driver was fortunate in not even having to try to understand. "To the Morris house. If you see a woman in the garden, stop before you come to it. I want to talk to the woman known locally as Mrs. Morris."

Roakes was efficient as a driver. He started the car and drove there. He did not say he knew the name.

So they were going back to their beginnings, Ball thought. Either it was the desperate cast of a man who knew he was wrong by now (since all groups of people had difficulties in their lives, just as the Trequayne estate people had, but that did not necessarily make them murderers, even though the murder was in their midst), or Brentford had seen something that Ball had not.

Ball preferred to think the latter, though like all people who did not see things, he did not quite believe it. Pure logical deduction, he wondered, or something difficult, like the human situation, that frowned-upon branch of police work which suggested you might arrive at a conclusion by knowing people? He would soon find out.

The driver took them down the drive towards the entrance to the estate, then back along the Morris drive, circling round the area of land that the path on which they had found the nightdress must cut across. They glimpsed the Silcrest house in passing, where the parents, Ball guessed must still be in agony, thinking "For her to die like that!" Then the driver went slowly as they approached the Morris house.

Betty Keen was in the garden. The driver stopped, and they watched her through the bushes. At least she had not lied to Brentford about one thing. She was interested in gardening, for, whatever was happening on the rest of the estate, she was peacefully and quietly using the late afternoon to spray the roses in a rose bed.

They sat and watched her working with a syringe and bucket, delicately turning the syringe up to spray beneath the leaves, then bending down again to fill it from the bucket. She was quite alone. The birds were mostly silent since it was far too early yet for their evening song, but she might have had no other company on the estate.

"Come on," Brentford said to Ball.

They left the car and went through the bushes to her. They were near her before she saw them, and by then it was too late for her to avoid them. She stood among the roses, trapped by her equipment but unable to look as though she were going somewhere else.

When they came near her, she looked at them and said: "William is inside if you wish to speak to him."

It was possible that Brentford did wish to speak to William, Ball realised, but not just yet. At the moment he was looking at Betty Keen as though she were some kind of puzzle, a box perhaps, of which he must find the key before it could be unlocked.

He looked at her syringe and bucket. "You use a spray, not D.D.T. dust?" he asked her.

She was suspicious. She did not look as though she really believed that the questions he wished to ask her would be about gardening.

"I use a spray."

"Why?" It was Brentford who looked as though he had paused on the way to going somewhere else, to see Morris perhaps. "Isn't the dust cleaner, and more effective?"

Ball watched her look resentful and then begin to look resigned. She was not truly evasive, he thought. It was just that there was a barrier. They had made a mistake when they had first met her. They had elucidated the fact that she was living unmarried with William Morris. It had not been wise. Get over and beyond that, and she might prove to be a different kind of person.

She frowned at Brentford, but she gave him her answer. "I like a garden to be a garden. With birds and insects. I don't grow flowers for show, you know."

They thought about her answer.

Brentford spoke mildly: "Why are you so reticent, Miss Keen?"

She tensed. "Am I?"

Brentford nodded. But he did not seem critical, only curious.

"When I spoke to you this morning, you could very easily have told me about David Feltham and Miss Silcrest, could you not?"

She looked troubled.

"Her father told me almost at once," he said. "If he had not, others would. What did you gain by it?"

Her troubled expression changed. She stood for a moment with the syringe in her hands, then shook her head.

"I didn't want to mislead you." She sounded oddly definite.

Brentford looked at her steadily. He seemed to accept her statement that she did not wish to mislead him. But he said, again not critically, only wishing to know:

"Was that why, as soon as we were gone, you got on to the phone to David Feltham and warned him about us and the finding of the body?"

Ball realised with a shock that Brentford could indeed have been critical about that. He himself had almost forgotten Feltham's early evidence.

She looked defensive and evasive again.

"Was it unnatural for me to phone the neighbours after what happened here this morning?"

To Ball's surprise she did not make the implied statement as though she expected it to be believed. It was rather as though she were testing out Brentford. For what, he wondered? To see if he were harmless?

"Miss Keen," said Brentford gently. "You didn't phone the neighbours. The Trueman-Davies learned of the murder from a tradesman's van. The only person you phoned was David Feltham."

Ball watched while she realised, as he himself had to do a little, that while Brentford might be harmless, he was not, at least, stupid.

She laid down her syringe in her bucket.

Watching her, Ball thought quietly, but with astonishment: he's done it.

She took more time putting her syringe in the bucket than was strictly necessary, and then she wiped her hands. Brentford gave her the time. Unlike that morning, he did not attempt to hurry her.

She turned and looked sideways at him while wiping her hands on a clump of grass she plucked.

"I can tell you this about David," she said. "He didn't do it."

Evenly, Brentford said: "You know that?"

She thought about it, as though it were necessary to answer him quite exactly. Perhaps, Ball thought it was a thing she had learned about Brentford, as he had, in the last two minutes.

"I know him," she said.

"Well?" said Brentford.

She looked at him passively, wondering apparently how much was implied by his question as to whether she knew Feltham well. Then she came out from among the rose bushes. She began to walk across the lawn. When they saw where she was going, they followed her.

There was a rustic seat on the lawn, and she went to sit on it rather as she might lead a guest to it at a garden party or social gathering.

143

But what she said was different.

"I was married," she said, looking up seriously at Brentford as he arrived with her, "don't laugh, to a Mr. Smithers."

Which did not sound like a breakthrough, Ball thought, since what Betty Keen had to say otherwise was wholly negative.

CHAPTER TWENTY-EIGHT

"When was this?" said Brentford. Betty Keen had sat in one corner of the rustic seat on the edge of the lawn, and indicated the other corner to him. With some slight evident doubt about its cleanliness, he looked at it and sat on it.

Ball made himself inconspicuous, walking round the seat before he took out his notebook. It was not the kind of thing that passed Betty Keen however. She turned and looked at him gravely as soon as he began to write in it.

"Seven years ago, I married him."

"He's here?" Brentford looked around the estate. "I mean he's somewhere round here?"

"As far as I am aware he is in Australia or New Zealand."

Brentford looked the obvious question as to why she had mentioned him at all, or perhaps was just expectant.

"It was a marriage that went wrong, Inspector. You may not think that that was very serious, but it was. My parents were old-fashioned. They had not had me educated for any career but marriage. And it was my second marriage. My second childless marriage, which is significant, and it went wrong."

Brentford found difficulty in countering her tone, which was formal to the point of complacency, and self-assured.

"You suggest that it was the fact that you were childless——" His tone was dry.

"What I suggest," she said, "is that, with my second marriage going wrong, as the first had done, and finding myself childless, I consulted David Feltham."

Brentford frowned. She made it sound too clear and easy. And fairly pointless.

"What is wrong with that?" she asked him. "This was before I knew any of the other people here. I consulted David, who introduced me to George Silcrest later, and through him I met William." She sounded mildly interesting.

Brentford said : "People who consulted Mr. Feltham seem to have had a tendency to become his friends, which isn't common in normal practice."

She nodded, accepting it. "Yes, but that is what he was like. He is—unfortunate. That is what I have to tell you."

Ball wondered. It hardly seemed possible that she could tell them more about David Feltham. After Brentford's last talk with him, it seemed they knew him whole.

But Brentford spoke to Betty Keen as though they knew very little: "What I know of him officially is that he retired exceptionally early."

She looked at him steadily. "They do, don't they?" she said. "Gynaecologists who make friends of their patients, women."

Brentford paused: "You mean——?"

She shook her head with unexpected calm.

"No. Oddly enough, not quite like that. There was talk of course. David seemed to invite it, didn't he? He surrounded himself with talk. Professionally, that he got away with murder. But it was just talk. I ceased to be a patient before he made a friend of me. There was no unprofessional conduct. And my marriage was already on the rocks before I tried to have an affair with him."

She was so clear and cool that Brentford looked hard at her.

"I said 'tried'," she reminded him. "In fact it was neither the talk not his conduct that spoiled his high career."

"What did?" said Brentford evenly.

She looked back at him unflinching. "I told you he was a remarkable man. Look at it from my point of view. My marriage was breaking down again. I was desperate and did not know which way to turn. David was one of the few reasonably wealthy, unattached, eligible men I knew. I told myself I was in love with him. It is possible I behaved ridiculously. I certainly flung myself at him and put myself in a compromising position with him." It was surprising how frank she could be.

Brentford's narrowed eyes wondered visibly why she was telling him all this.

"I discovered then why he allowed the talk and encouraged it," she said. She looked at him dryly. "Why he allowed it to be said about him that he was a boy with women. There was only one reason. I was innocent perhaps not to have suspected it. It is not so unusual in a man who invited that kind of talk."

She paused, giving them time to soak up her words, looking at Brentford to see if he had fully absorbed her meaning, and why she had not spoken earlier.

Brentford considered what she said and would not let her get away with the implication so easily. "It is hardly believable," he said quietly. "A man in his position. A man who would be expected to know most about things like that, even if he had specialised on the women's side."

"Yes!" she said, and the word was harsh and she said it sharply. She let them see she felt it.

"You have evidence of this?" Brentford was quiet.

"Inspector, you are a fool if you think I am going to give you chapter and verse and times and dates!"

"Then why am I to believe you, and how did it end his career?" said Brentford.

She looked at him pensively, and shook her head.

"If you can't see it, then I can't help you, Inspector. Logically, there was no reason. There is no reason why an impotent man should not be a gynaecologist. Probably some are."

The word "impotent", Ball thought. She could come out with it in plain language. It was surprising how little reticent Betty Keen could be.

Brentford thought about it, visibly trying to connect the two things, the man's sex life and his career as a consultant surgeon. But it was not possible to do it in the abstract, Ball himself suddenly realised. You had to do it in terms of what they knew of David Feltham.

146

"I believe I can see," said Brentford. "If this was something he discovered..." He looked at her as though he were about to say "in the course of an affair with you", but he changed it to: "at the height of his career. When he should in fact have been feeling at the height of his powers." He thought: "It might," he said, "have an effect on his confidence."

She ignored what it was possible that he had been about to say.

"It was," she said, "and it did."

"You mean that because of this he lost confidence as a surgeon?"

"I mean it changed his life."

It had, Ball thought. The time she was speaking of could only be that when Feltham had begun to take an interest not in the physiology of adult women but in the psychology of Caroline Silcrest, then a girl of tender years.

If Betty Keen had given them nothing else, she had given them an insight into the background of Feltham's story, and had made it clear it was a tragic one.

And something else followed.

"You do understand now, Inspector, why I did not direct your attention this morning to David Feltham?"

"Yes," Brentford said, "I do." He thought it out and carefully defined it: "You saw at once that, in view of his association with Caroline, we would suspect him, especially if she proved to have been with him the night before."

He added: "And you knew quite well that he would not murder her for any of the usual reasons."

Ball saw what he meant at once. Brentford had begun, as was inevitable, by suspecting Feltham of having murdered Caroline for what he himself had defined as the normal reasons: because she would not sleep with him, or because she had slept with him, as a fact to be concealed. More recently, he had taken a further step, putting to Feltham the other reason: because she would sleep with him, and he was tempted by her.

What he was saying now, unknown to Betty Keen, was that there was another reason, a further step. If Caroline had thrown herself at Feltham, and he had rejected her because he

147

must, then another situation arose: that the girl suspected the reason for her rejection. Ball's imagination was not normally vivid, but he saw it suddenly, the girl being thrown out, literally pushed from the house by Feltham, and turning round, at the door perhaps, before she went off into the moonlight, saying: "You won't have me? Then I know why. It's because you can't!" And Feltham, watching her go, would know that Caroline, least of all, was a girl to keep her tongue still. But was that enough?

Brentford's confirmation of what Betty Keen thought was carefully worded not to include humiliation and frustration as the causes of an anger that might have sent Feltham following her, as Brentford had suggested, to head her off as she fled from him through the night. He looked quickly from his notebook at her.

But Betty Keen was looking at Brentford coolly. She said: "No, Inspector."

What Betty Keen said then seemed to indicate, if it were true, that they had been wasting their time for the greater part of that day: quite apart from Crawford's point.

"What I meant, Inspector, was that David would not have murdered Caroline at all. In fact, I am sure he did not. You see, he hasn't got it in him."

Betty Keen got up then, having said what she had to say.

She looked at Brentford for a moment, and walked away from him, back towards her roses.

Which, as Ball had seen, was wholly negative.

CHAPTER TWENTY-NINE

So there it was, Ball thought as Brentford got up from the seat where he had been sitting by Betty Keen and they walked across the lawn. They were engaged on a process of elimination now, and what was left? The Trueman-Davies stories?

Brentford had not even pretended to believe in what Tessa

Trueman-Davies told him, at least in its entirety or most essential details. And they were walking on only towards the Morris house.

Where Morris, as Brentford himself had said, had only been evasive to them about where he had been the previous night because he had been with Helen Silcrest.

"Do you think he is in?" Ball said, from lack of anything else to say. He shielded his eyes against the glare of the sinking sun and peered at the glass-fronted house as though, which he did not believe, they would find a quarry there.

If any existed on the estate.

Brentford walked on to the house as though it were inevitable that they would go there, though when they had arrived he had spoken only of Betty Keen. He seemed surer now.

"He is," said Brentford, and sure enough they glimpsed Morris then, sitting not far from the large plate-glass window in an easy chair, with a whisky glass beside him, and looking out.

Ball did not know whether the slight sense of inevitability that he felt was due to the fact that Betty Keen had said the man was there, or because Brentford had turned unhesitatingly in that direction.

In fact Ball looked with a slight frown at Morris as they approached the house. He had not come out to meet them and he seemed content to sit there and let Betty Keen do all the gardening. He was a reticent man, he thought, and he wondered what Brentford would get out of him.

They went up on the terrace and round and through the door, finding it open to the evening air. The tour brought Morris's back to them. He did not turn to see them. He did not move at all until they were in the room behind him, and then, in a voice that was no more than an acknowledgement, he said: "Hello, Inspector."

Brentford did not reply to the greeting. He continued walking in without invitation, looked around when he came abreast of Morris, and chose a chair.

He sat down in it with care, as though he expected to stay a long time. Ball registered the signs and chose a comfortable chair for himself. They sat down quite, he realised as he did it, as though they had come to spend the evening.

149

"You'll have a whisky, Inspector?" Morris said. He had looked at them and then looked out of the window again.

"No," said Brentford, but without the slightest implication.

The conversation hung fire. The two men, the thick one looking out of the window and the tall one watching him without expression, seemed to wait for the other to make the opening moves.

Morris turned his head and looked at Brentford.

"I suppose you want to ask me again where I was last night?"

"Among other things," said Brentford.

Morris continued to look at him.

"Helen was here, you know," he said. "She stayed until about eleven, and then I took her part-way home. It was all perfectly innocent."

For some reason it was Brentford who now looked out of the window. They could see Betty Keen working on the roses. She had not offered to come in. Nor, Ball remembered, had she herself said anything about what had happened the previous night.

Brentford should have questioned everyone far more closely about these times, Ball thought. What had they? After their first visit to the house that morning, Brentford had told Ball that Silcrest had said that he and his wife had got back "around midnight". That might be any time between eleven and one. If Brentford insisted on staying on the estate, it was the obvious point to clear up. Except perhaps that it would be unusually difficult to tell if any particular person were telling the truth. . . .

"Just you and Betty Keen and Helen Silcrest," Brentford said. "What did you do, talk?"

"As a matter of fact we played three-handed whist."

"Whist? Why not bridge?"

Morris coloured slightly, and Ball wondered how Brentford could possibly have got to a point that touched him so very soon.

"Helen doesn't like bridge," Morris said.

"I thought not," Brentford said, turning from the window to him. "From what I saw of her, she doesn't look as though she

150

would have the temperament, while you and Betty Keen would be very good."

We are talking about whist and bridge, Ball thought. We are talking about parlour games.

"That's what I wanted to ask you about," Brentford said.

Morris said: "What?" For no reason that Ball could see, he looked defensive.

Ball himself wondered what Helen Silcrest's whist-playing habits could have to do with that or any other case.

But Brentford, looking at Morris steadily, said:

"Your relations with George and Helen Silcrest?"

Morris sat silent. It was odd, Ball thought.

It was almost a new feature of the case, for he could see no reason for Morris's expression. No reason at all why Morris, sitting there, should look not only resentful, which was normal, but also defensive, trapped.

CHAPTER THIRTY

Yet it began easily and simply enough.

Morris looked hard at Brentford and said easily, too easily perhaps since his resentful expression remained and he coloured slightly: "My relations with George Silcrest are business ones."

Brentford sat silent, not even saying that that was not enough.

Morris sat up. He made a relatively lengthy statement to dismiss the matter.

"I met George Silcrest during the war. We came out together. You know how it is. George had a job to go back to. I wanted to set up in business on my own. He lent me his war gratuity. Later, I paid him back."

Not a very long statement, Ball thought, after all. Not at least in view of the intricacies they had already heard about in connection with the Trequayne estate. He looked around again at Morris's pleasant house and spacious room. A war gratuity was what, a few hundred pounds?

"All right, go on, please, Mr. Morris," said Brentford.

Morris looked resentful. "I told you. He lent me three hundred pounds. And I worked. Damn it, there's no secret about it! When we eventually sold the factory, his share was fifteen thousand."

He gave the figure aggressively.

"Tell me about that," said Brentford.

Morris looked as though he would not speak at all.

"To make fifteen thousand out of three hundred is a long way to go," said Brentford reasonably. "You must see I want to hear about it."

Ball thought, with quiet amazement: yes, reasonable.

Morris did not seem to think so.

"For God's sake, it was normal, Inspector! I set up in light engineering. Why not? It was what my namesake, William Morris who became Lord Nuffield, had done. And when I saw a profitable line, as he had done, I went into it. Only I went into plastics."

Perhaps people on the Trequayne estate had different ideas of financial normality, Ball thought.

"Why plastics?" Brentford said in his reasonable tone again.

"Because there's not much you can do in a backyard machineshop. I had an order for plastic presses and moulds and I saw it was more profitable to use the moulds than make them, and buy the plastics and raw materials."

"More capital?" said Brentford.

Morris looked hard at him and said: "Not from George Silcrest."

"Not when you expanded?"

"Silcrest was getting married at that time. He wanted to take his money out, not put more in. He couldn't. I had to get more from other sources. We went on expanding."

Brentford looked at him closely. "If you were in a position to expand, why could not Silcrest take his money out?" His question was sharp and searching.

Morris looked straight back at him.

"You don't know much about business, do you? In a virtually new industry, which plastics was, you don't expand because you want to. You do it because you must. Because machines and processes are improving all the time. If you don't buy new machines, and lower costs, your competitors will. You will be out, producing third rate goods at a high price. You have to improve and produce on a larger scale all the time. Have you ever heard of the rat race? Silcrest could have taken his money out, but if he had, as I told him, he would have put the firm in the hands of the receivers."

"So what it amounted to was that although Silcrest was making money fast on paper, he couldn't touch it?"

Morris said stiffly: "Yes. It was that!"

"You were a limited company? He could sell his shares?" Brentford was sharp again.

"I told you. I asked him not to."

Brentford was silent for a moment and then said:

"Yet you did sell. You sold right out, disposed of the firm, and retired to this estate. That's what we're coming to, isn't it, that you never did become Lord Nuffield?"

Morris winced. Ball watched him with surprise.

"That was Silcrest?" Brentford said. "He did that?" He watched every expression on Morris's face.

Morris looked at him with an expression of suffering.

"Tell me about it," Brentford said, persuasively.

For a moment, Ball thought that Morris would not. Then he said: "You could equally blame it on the City."

Brentford waited. Morris looked grim and sad, then angry.

"The City!" Morris said. "The Old School Ties! If they are in difficulty, they call on an uncle or someone who went to the same school to put on the pressure, to hold back a promised million loan. 'Their word is their bond' they say of London businessmen! You know what that means? They put nothing down on paper. You ask the Excise! The man runs a Rolls, but you ask him and he hasn't got an income. He lives on capital gains and nothing else——"

"George Silcrest," said Brentford. He sounded patient.

"I'm telling you! It came at a bad time, that's all. Maybe the City had learned something since the first William Morris.

153

Hell, we weren't as big as that!" Morris himself looked round his room and the interior of his house as though measuring his wealth by it. "Our new factory in the East End. Give us another ten years and then——! But they struck earlier than they had with the original William Morris. A man came into my office one day and looked out at the view as though he owned it. 'You've read the *Financial Times*?' he said. 'Rationalisation in the Plastics Industry?' He turned round to my desk. 'Vertical amalgamation, that is the thing.' I knew what that meant. The same consortium wanted to own the whole process from the chemical raw materials to the finished product, and I had been having trouble with my suppliers." He stopped, and stared at Brentford.

"And that was when Silcrest decided to pull out?" said Brentford.

"I'm telling you!" said Morris. "It was a take-over. They made an offer and gave me a week. I called an emergency board meeting and put it to them. It meant a fight, I said. We were not going to be right out of supplies; I could import them from a firm in Holland. But it meant a long hard struggle. It was no use having any illusions. It would be a year or two before they or we came out on top. And George Silcrest was at that board meeting. He proposed an adjournment motion. A day to think about it, he said. I wondered what he was up to. He told me. He came round to the new flat I had recently moved into with Betty Keen, and told me his story.

Brentford nodded, and Morris scowled at him.

When he spoke again it was with a difficulty that contrasted with the ease and assurance with which he had told the business details:

"I didn't really know George. We had been business partners. Board meetings, an occasional office conference, and sometimes a night out. It was on a night out that he introduced me to Betty Keen. But that kind of thing doesn't bring you into contact with the wife and family. When he began to tell me about them, it was almost news to me. It seemed that when he had been asking for his money, it hadn't been just the normal inclination to make a killing and get out, as I had thought. He had a girl who had been giving him a lot of trouble. He gave me the ghastly details. One school after another, and all of them more expensive. Doctors, advice from specialists. He had not been getting on too well with his wife, either. There had been another woman, and that had cost him more. But the real crux was his son. He was really a problem, a mental case. And yet George wouldn't let him go. For some inexpressible reason, he loved that son. Couldn't bear to send him to an asylum, which was what it would come to, as he grew older, if they kept him there in London. He told me he would do anything rather than that, and he had been casting round. What he needed was a place in the country, not a big place, but private and with ample grounds. And of course money to live on, some way of cashing in his assets, since looking after this son was going to be a full-time job. And he told me he had found it. This estate. In his estate-agent business he had been able to pick up the option cheap, and it was ripe for development. He could turn it into a place some people would give their eyes for. The capital gain on development alone would put him in the clear, and he would set himself up for life. If he could do it. He didn't know if he could. But he was going to try. If it was a choice between me and his son, it had to be his son."

Brentford looked at Morris carefully. "In fact, he had to have his money?"

Morris was silent, looking away from out of the window, for a moment. Then his tone was quiet.

"It was more than that," he said. "He was the one who had given me my start. Without him, I'd have been a ten or twenty pound a week man. And he needed help. It was something that came through nakedly, through everything he said. And I couldn't do anything about it. He said he needed his money, and he did. He was going to have to sell anyway, and that meant that the consortium would get their foot in. It would be one of their men who would be on my board of directors now, with the voting powers that came from owning a heavy block of shares. I could see that I might last a few years, but I would be fighting a losing battle. And so I did the big thing."

"You sold out?" said Brentford as quietly.

"I told him I would accept the consortium's offer. And I

would do more....I hadn't forgotten what he had done for me. I would look into this scheme of his. If it was as sound as he said it was, I would put my own money in and make sure it was the success he dreamed of. No one, least of all him, was going to regret having lent their money to William Morris." The voice was even.

Morris concluded his story of his business relations with George Silcrest and sat looking out of the window.

But it was strange, Ball thought. He had told a story he might rightfully tell with pride, but he had not told it that way, surprisingly, to Brentford.

Instead, he sat looking out of the window with an expression of bitterness and regret. Perhaps he was off guard at that moment, for his expression was as though he had done a thing he was ashamed of, or perhaps regretted.

CHAPTER THIRTY-ONE

It did not go the way Ball expected.

So what have we got, thought Ball.

He looked at Morris, who had, after having told his story, lost something of his first resentment.

A businessman's story, he thought. And not even, as Brentford had perhaps been hoping, any quarrels, nefarious dealings, or debts unsettled.

Nothing, in fact.

Or was it nothing, the emotion that Morris showed?

It was hardly likely, and never had been likely, that Caroline Silcrest had been killed for money. From desire perhaps, or fear, or anger. It had to be one of the emotions.

But Ball did not expect Brentford's next words.

He said: "Go on."

And Morris, turning to him, which Ball found strange, looked as though he did expect them.

Expected them and feared them. Of course, Ball thought.

For the story had not, after all, stopped five years ago. It had stopped last night in the woods. If, that was, it had ever stopped.

Brentford had spoken of "treating the case as though the girl were alive", as though the story were still going on.

Morris looked defensive again; not quite so resentful, but even more defensive, as he said: "Go on to where?"

He was only pretending now, and not very well, that he had told it all.

They waited.

"I said I've told you," Morris said.

But they had lived five years since then, Ball thought. Not merely that. It was not merely the passage of time. They had lived together since then.

In an isolated community on the Trequayne estate.

"I asked you about your relations with George and Helen Silcrest," Brentford said.

"And I said I told you."

"You've told me about your business relations only," Brentford said.

Which was the point perhaps, Ball saw.

Since the main part of the story would come after they had come to live together, and not before.

Who had told them what had happened since they had come to live on the Trequayne estate? Feltham had. And Tessa had done so, and Penny Trueman-Davies had done so partly. Which was not enough.

There was a tendency, to which Brentford, and even Ball, was alive now, to avoid the present.

"What other relations are there?" Morris said.

"Friendship?" Brentford suggested.

Morris seemed to resent it.

"You can't tell a story like that. And would you describe it as 'a relation'?"

Brentford looked back quietly at the man who was splitting hairs.

"A man who is the lover of his best friend's wife may be said to stand in a relation to the family," he said.

Morris coloured.

It was no good, Ball saw. Morris would have to tell the story.

"My relations with Helen have been perfectly honourable," Morris said unexpectedly. "Do you think I would have kept Betty here otherwise? Do you think I would have gone on living with one woman to whom I was not married if I had been 'lover', in the sense you use it, to another?"

He was indignant and aggressive.

"That is what I mean," said Brentford. "That is what puzzled me. That Betty," he looked out of the window at her, "should be so content and settled here, and, despite her awareness of your interest in Helen Silcrest, ready to play whist, I think you said it was, with her, and to cultivate your garden with a view to next year."

"I don't understand? What are you saying? You are accusing me because my affection for my best friend's wife, if you call him that, is innocent?"

"Affection?" said Brentford.

Morris was irate and angry: "Pity, then!"

Brentford stopped and looked at him.

It was odd, Ball thought, what importance he seemed to attach to that single word, pity.

Morris looked at him stupefied, as though he truly did not understand.

"Why should you feel pity, pity amounting to love, for Helen Silcrest?" Brentford asked.

"Dammit, you can see why! Her children——!"

"Her children, not her husband?"

Morris said, as though it were all too difficult for him: "Oh, hell——!"

"There is at least one person on the estate who takes an extremely poor view of Helen Silcrest's husband," Brentford said. Something cold and inexorable crept into his tone. "It did not seem to me that you were too happy to have sacrificed yourself, your desire to emulate Lord Nuffield, and to have done the big thing, I think you called it, for Caroline Silcrest's father."

"What the hell? Who criticised——?"

"What do you really think of George Silcrest?" Brentford said.

Morris seemed to shrink a little, Ball noticed, to hunch his shoulders.

"Why?" said Brentford. "Why are you sorry you did 'the big thing' for George Silcrest? You knew him, didn't you? Or has he changed since then?"

Morris still did not answer, but he looked as though he wished to, Ball saw with surprise. He looked as though he were suffering.

"Or was it that you found out about him, discovered what kind of a man he was, after you came here?" Brentford said.

Ball tried hard to catch the fleeting expression on Morris's face. He had nothing to write in his notebook so long as Morris did not answer, and he could watch. It was to interpret that flash that was another matter.

Morris looked for an instant, Ball thought with surprise, as though not he, but Brentford, knew something about George Silcrest. It was that to which he seemed to attach importance. That Brentford knew it: so that he, Morris would not have to be the one to—what? To point a finger?

It was astonishing what a difference it seemed to make.

But it was Brentford himself who startled Ball.

Quite quietly he said something that had been obvious, or should have been obvious, all that day. Yet it was shocking how, when it was said in words, it stood out sharp and etched and clear in Ball's mind.

"I came on to this estate this morning, Morris. Let me tell you. I found what? A dead girl. A girl who did not look as though she had been raped, but only strangled. And a girl who was still a child. And, Morris, almost the first thing I learned was that there was insanity in her family."

Ball thought: "No—he can't mean——" then watched Morris's eyes widen.

Brentford watched him, then spoke with thought.

"It's difficult being a policeman, Morris. Especially a policeman intruding in an estate like this. Have you ever thought what it is, a policeman's role? We see people. A woman bereaved, perhaps. Her behaviour may be normal. We don't know. We can hardly intrude on her grief by saying 'Just why did you say that?' Not at such a time. Not then and there."

Brentford's voice was softer.

It was another thing—that Brentford was no longer driving Morris but persuading him—that startled Ball.

"And so," said Brentford, looking at Morris, "we ask the neighbours." He looked at Morris closely. "We ask the ones who ought to know. Why she was lying. Why she was evasive."

Ball felt misled. It took time, after so long, to realise the implications of this line of Brentford's.

This direct line, in which Brentford was talking quite calmly of what he had seen, observed, and wondered about so early that it was even before he had been to Feltham's.

It was something that must have been in his mind all day, even from the time of his decision to stay on the estate, yet simple, so simple, particularly since it had nothing to do with Feltham.

It was—if it was to be believed, Ball thought, this suggestion Brentford was making—as though he had seen what Feltham had told him, and the Trueman-Davies, and now Morris, as about the Silcrests. A common factor, if it was to be believed. A common factor of reluctance. . . .

"It's something awkward, for a start," Brentford told Morris, "to go around asking people about their friends. And there are things that make it worse. The odd ideas, the fixed ideas that people have, on police and crime. Do you know that? That the people feel we are apart, experts in the unknown, in finding those strange unlikely creatures, whose nature it is, since they are called criminals, to commit all crimes. Naturally, you don't know them. In a place like this, we have that to contend with, for a start."

Brentford was talking, Ball saw, as though he were giving an idle lecture, or passing time. But every word he said, to judge by Morris's increasingly agonised and tortured expression, had a deep significance to him.

"People," Brentford said, "even people like you, Morris, get their ideas of crime and criminals from books. Even particularly people like you, whose reading is probably confined to thrillers.

And it's a pity, that. Because while thrillers picture criminals as ingenious and desperate characters, they usually aren't. Take murder, for instance. Child murder in particular. The newspapers make a great to-do about the number of children who are killed and raped by strangers. But in fact it isn't like that at all. Have you ever heard the saying that 'murder is a family crime'? It makes it sound quite homely. But then it is homely. By far the greatest number of child-murders everywhere are committed—by the parents. The child's own parents, and not by friends and relatives even. You might almost take it as a human law. If it isn't a stranger it must be the parents. As policemen, we have to know and think that."

Morris looked horrified and Brentford said: "Especially bad and exasperating children. Naturally they are most murdered. And if there is insanity in the family too, the position is such, statistically you understand, that it's hardly worth even looking for a stranger."

Brentford looked at Morris and said: "Was it George or Helen Silcrest who murdered Caroline, Morris? You know why I am asking you. Because you are the one who has known them longest, and you are the one who will know!" His voice had tensed and then unleashed.

Brentford was not even accusing Morris of murder, Ball saw, surprised. But of something else.

And Morris said: "No!"

CHAPTER THIRTY-TWO

Ball sat amazed at two things.

He was a blunt man, Ball thought. A man who had worked his way up. And now he had a spacious house, on a beautiful estate, and a woman in the garden who was loyal.

A man like that, Morris seemed to indicate, should not be asked to betray his friends. If that was it.

If that was it about Feltham and the Trueman-Davies's too,

who had talked almost exclusively about themselves. Usually in such a case people were full of wild speculations about who the murderer was. They had theories, the famous sex-mad stranger....

But to say they knew who was not to say whom they knew.

Except that he, Ball, when he had seen the body, had thought too: a high romantic crime. And now it was not like that.

Morris knew, Ball thought. But what had they? The proposition that he would either tell them or he would not, or that, because he knew what the crime was, he would try deliberately to mislead them.

It was up to them, with him there before them, to know which it was that he was doing.

The parents, for instance. He said it was not the parents. They had cause enough, because they were unfortunate. Unfortunate people always had been guilty people in police eyes. But Morris said no, and Brentford, if only from policy, had to pretend not to believe him.

Brentford spoke almost innocently.

"He or she?" he said. "Which one of them has had the worst time?" It was not new to him.

Morris looked out of his window, gazing across his pleasant garden in the direction of the Silcrest house.

It was as though he were chained there, Ball thought. Unlike Betty Keen, he could not find escape in an easy activity, like gardening. While Ball himself thought: No.

"Helen," said Morris, "is a little unbalanced. I suppose you saw that?" His voice was unsteady now.

Ball thought back to the time they had seen Helen Silcrest in that same room. Unbalanced, he thought? Perhaps. But then she had been a woman who had lost a daughter. Or had she? When she had first been there she had not lost one but temporarily mislaid one. She had behaved how? As though she knew the girl was dead? Brentford had noted that, no doubt, or perhaps that she was unbalanced. But how little could a man like Morris say?

Brentford nodded. Helen Silcrest had lied.

"George Silcrest told me at that same time, before we came

162

here," Morris said. "She had an uncle in an asylum and a grandfather who committed suicide. He didn't know that before they married." He sounded anguished.

But then people usually didn't, Ball thought. Few young men in love, and least of all those recently back from the war, made proper inquiries about their wife's family.

Brentford did not speak. He had said enough.

"George had an eye for a beautiful woman," Morris said. "I told you he told me he had two of them."

Brentford did speak then.

"How open was he? What sort of an understanding did he give you of how he was working and planning this estate?" His tone was careful.

Morris looked, once again, as though the shadow of reticence was passing across his face.

But perhaps that was it. He knew his own nature. He knew that there were some things it was not in him to be able to conceal.

"I did know him fairly well, you see. When Betty, who was listening to our conversation, said, 'An estate with open gardens? I would like that,' I thought I knew. Why, he had introduced Betty to me. As a gift almost. He had been preparing the ground. For my retirement to the estate. I wouldn't put it past him."

That was the way it was, Ball thought. It had the unfortunate ring of truth. People were like that. They did things of which you could not think them capable, then wondered why you thought them capable. There just was no motiveless action, or if there was, then someone would attribute a motive.

But there was something else. They were not neglible on the Trequayne estate, neither in what they saw nor in what they forgave.

"And the others? Did he tell you what he was doing to Trueman-Davies?"

Morris looked as though then, in the past, it had worried him.

"Yes. But it was later. When he had to introduce them to me and I had already met Penny. He told me of the—arrangement they were making. He and Henry. Henry Trueman-

163

Davies was no fool. They got Feltham to introduce the estate to him, but he'd seen. As soon as he saw Penny and George together: 'You two already know one another well?' Henry knew. But George knew Henry. Knowing is a different matter from letting anyone know he knows what goes on between his wife and George. And George saw that."

Looking at Morris, Brentford said: "The daughter knows."

"Yes. He knows she knows. But that doesn't imply he'll let her know he knows she knows!"

Brentford looked at Morris as though asking him what kind of a life was that.

And Morris looked away.

"And yet," said Brentford, looking at Morris more narrowly still, "although George Silcrest was so honest with you, you were still shocked by him when you came here and got to know him better?"

Morris turned from the window to give him a look of suffering. He tried to fight, and failed.

"He did something unforgivable. I only found out from Helen."

Brentford said quietly: "To her, you mean?"

Morris paused before he spoke.

"You can see it from his point of view. He had married and had a normal life. Then he found that instead of sane, healthy children he had got sick and partly mad ones. And his wife, in his view, was the one to blame. Not that he ceased to support her or ever did less than his duty by her or the children. He was, actually, wrecking his life and career for them. But she was, so far as he was concerned, mad, and a source of madness. To live with her was a torture to him. And so, when he produced the estate plan, for her and the children, he did not tell her everything. Maybe his feeling about her made him incapable of it by then. He just told her about the estate and a plan to retire to the country with the children. Naturally, she was delighted. She had been madly jealous of Penny, and she imagined Penny would be left behind. As soon as she heard of the plan, she put her money, every penny and household savings into the estate, and he allowed her. Then, when she got here, and actually met the 'Mrs. Trueman-Davies' she had heard about, whom she hadn't met till then, she discovered it was Penny. She accused him of treachery, and while he did not say it, he more or less intimated that since she was like her children and uncle and suicidal grandfather, and he was doing so much for her, because of that she could not expect the consideration, also, given to a normal human being."

Morris looked sick and haunted.

A twist, Ball thought. The claws at last. And then he corrected himself. Morris had not yet said whether he saw George or Helen Silcrest, the bad one or the mad one, as the murderer of the child. He said neither.

Brentford looked at Morris quietly.

"Helen is still an attractive woman," he said.

"Yes."

"For her to tell you that story, you would have had to know her intimately."

Morris looked down.

"I myself hadn't thought much of the way George had worked me and Henry and David into the estate. Not that there was anything wrong with it. It was perfectly genuine, and everything he said. But to David Feltham, he had said, 'I would appreciate it if you could take an interest and come with us to be near our daughter.'"

Brentford took a moral, policeman's line: "Offering him his daughter in fact?"

"No! That would have been all right! If he had let David bring her up, who knows? He's as mad as she is. He might have made a success of it. But George was not consistent. He began to take her away from David as soon as David began to do better with her than he did."

Ball watched Brentford looking at Morris with an expression he knew. It happened when a witness's testimony was tying up in detail with what they had already heard.

"But because you knew George better, you began to feel sympathy with Helen?" He dropped his voice a little. "Although, and despite the fact you knew all this about her and her family?"

Morris coloured again.

"I would never marry Helen!" he said. "Because of all this,

I would never allow myself to fall in love with her in that way. As Betty knows! As Betty knows quite well! Yet all the same..."

Brentford seized on the point, not quickly, but very deliberately, Ball saw.

"Yet all the same, what?"

Morris looked desperately uncomfortable.

"I did think—I had a talk with David once. About two years ago. About this madness that runs in families. I had only George's word about what it was and what it meant. But David confirmed it. It was not his branch, but he was able to tell me.... Only he said something more. Some technical point about recessive genes. It's the question you asked me. And the reason I felt sorry for Helen. It seems that to be really bad in the children it has to come from both sides...."

His face had gone crimson.

Brentford said: "You mean that Silcrest knows this?"

Morris shook his head. He had reached the limit, not of what he could but of what he would tell them.

"Does George Silcrest know what it means if his children are mad?" Brentford said. When Morris did not reply, he put it more plainly. "Does he know that he is as responsible and covered by his condemnation of her as she is? Morris! Does George Silcrest think that he may himself be mad?" His voice became suddenly sharp.

Morris simply sat and stared at him and either could not or would not speak.

Watching him carefully, Brentford said: "All right. Your sympathies are with Helen, Morris. But do you think it? That it was George who murdered Caroline?"

Ball closed his eyes, then looked at Brentford.

He watched Morris for a moment and then breathed out and said: "All right, don't answer that."

"I'll tell you this!" said Morris.

They watched him, his too visible expression as he made up his mind what, between loyalty to a friend and repressed love for the friend's wife, he could say.

"George is frightened," Morris said. "I don't mean necessarily what you just said. He's not necessarily afraid of going mad. Or even that he is mad, in some sense, if his children are. But think of what he has done for them. He was going up in the estate-agent world. He had a good business, good prospects, and trusted friends. And he sacrificed them all. An estate-agent, when he's offered a valuable property, doesn't beat the seller down and then buy himself. A friend doesn't use his friends. And a husband doesn't treat a wife as he treated Helen. But he did all these things and you can see what he's afraid of? He's had five years since then. Does it look to you that his sacrifice has been worth while?"

"I couldn't know a thing like that," said Brentford.

Morris looked at him grimly. "You could. You will, when you see his son, Clarence!"

"You mean——?"

"I don't mean," said Morris. He looked at the floor then up, beneath his brows at Brentford. "I can only tell you this. That George Silcrest has spent these five years on this estate watching his children, every day, for every sign of improvement or else of madness. Without interfering with them more than necessary, you understand. Because that would interfere with an observation that has looked to us like an obsession. You won't believe. Any tiny act they do, in the way of bad behaviour, now affects him as it would if a doctor told him he had a malignant cancer. And Helen told me this morning, when he was out and I took her home: he went out last night, she says. *She* says. After they went home and Caroline was missing. They knew she was missing. He said, she said, he'd look for her at Feltham's. And she was afraid. Afraid of what would happen if he caught her and Feltham together.... But he came back. Her story, you understand. To me, not you. He said he couldn't find her. Only he seemed quiet. He was no longer excited, as she was, by Caroline's absence, and frowned on her inquiries. Her natural inquiries, you might think, about where Caroline was, and what had happened to her——!"

Morris looked quickly at Brentford, then looked away.

Ball watched Brentford looking at Morris with that expression he knew, the one that confirmed that that was the way it had been, that it coincided with what he himself had seen, when he had heard George and Helen Silcrest's stories that morning, but not known then what was true, what acted, or the motive behind even true statements, that made them false. This was it, he thought.

But Brentford would not let Morris get away with it.

"And you knew all this this morning?" he said. "All of you. You knew the background. And when I came here now, you knew what she had said. But why? Morris, why are you shielding *him*?"

"No!" Morris said. He turned again. "Not know! Just guessed. That one or the other——! Don't you see how it is? That she will be accusing him, he her? And if one is right ... And what was I to do, anyone here? To guess? To tell you we don't know—we are sure, but only think——?"

Brentford was looking hard at Morris, who seemed to wish in vain to look away.

"Because after that——" said Morris. It came at last. "After I had taken her home, and he came back. He told me. You know, he had been to see the body. He said, 'I haven't told the Inspector yet, but she went out last night. And she's sick, Morris! You must have seen it. The children are not getting better. It has preyed on her mind. And though I don't think she knows she did it——!'"

Morris looked at them appalled. His mouth remained open for a moment as though still speaking. He said: "Poor Helen ... !" Then he looked at Brentford as though he were the man he envied least.

"You'll see when you go there," he said. "But you may know which one to believe. I don't! I did ... I don't..." He said: "Since they both accuse the other!"

Morris made a supreme effort and pulled himself together.

"You see that's it," he said. "That they both accuse the other. Because they're afraid. Because they think it might be. But don't you see? From the very fact they each accuse the other on equal grounds—it isn't either!"

CHAPTER THIRTY-THREE

No, thought Ball.

Brentford should not just sit there, accepting it, looking intent, as though he believed the story and its contradiction.

It wasn't right for Brentford to do that. He should lead on to something, to a solution now. He should say, sitting there, or getting up from his chair: "That's all very well, Morris, but I know for a fact that you..." Or Feltham. Or Betty Keen. Or Penny Trueman-Davies.

Brentford sat looking at Morris as though he assessed his soul. But he did not say: "Caroline accused you of raping her, Mr. Morris. You and Feltham. And, knowing what Silcrest was, that gave him ample scope for blackmail...."

Brentford did not seem to be thinking of anything as vague as that. He was thinking of something clear and definite.

Which in any event we, the police, are going to have to clear up, Ball suddenly thought.

Then Brentford moved. He said, "All right, Morris," and he said, "Come on," to Ball.

They got up and went slowly out of the room, onto the terrace, where they faced, Ball thought, as they looked at the view, the evening shadows, the pleasant prospect of the garden, with the sunset banking up, out over the creek and above the trees, the reality of murder now.

Brentford was waiting. So far as Ball could see, he was waiting for Betty Keen, who, seeing them appear, had dropped her gardening and was coming in.

He had a momentary hope. Brentford turned and spoke to him. "We had better not waste too much time. It's taken too long already." Then he went down to meet Betty Keen, who, a victim of the disadvantage of an open-plan house, had had to delay making dinner until the private interview was over.

"Where is the footpath to the Silcrest house?" Brentford asked her. "If you please, Miss Keen?"

She looked quietly at them. She knew, Ball thought. They

all did, only, with a murder in their midst, they would have said it was truer to say they guessed. She looked at the drive, where their car was, and then said, "Over there," and pointed to an opening in the bushes around the garden on the other side.

Brentford looked at it and spoke deliberately to Ball. "We'll walk." To Betty he said, "Thank you, Miss—Mrs. Morris."

There was something final about that, thought Ball, like the closing of an account with her, dismissive.

Ball wondered if it would be quicker, as Brentford led him across the garden, to walk, as Brentford proposed to do, along the murder route.

Or perhaps, like Ball, and despite what he had said, he wished to delay it a little longer.

The path, as they started along it quickly from the garden, must, however, be the one the murderer had used to bring the body to the creek, and the one Helen Silcrest had appeared from when she had arrived at the house that morning. But it was something more, Ball saw. Somewhere, between where they were and the Silcrests', it must join the path from Feltham's, and the route Crosston had been following when they left him, working on from where he had found the nightdress. Towards the murder point.

Above them in the branches, as they turned into the woods, the birds had begun their song, which they would keep up for two hours now as the beautiful evening turned to placid night.

CHAPTER THIRTY-FOUR

"It's here," Crosston said, and showed them.

The small, white sandal was jammed between two tree roots. It was not quite on the path, but a little off it, and the grass around it, quite clearly visible even in the shadowed light, was flattened for the distance of a yard.

Brentford looked back along the path down which he and

Ball had come. The junction with the track the girl had worn to Feltham's was twenty yards away in that direction.

"So she was," he said, "just going home...."

"Naked?" Crosston said.

"It looks like it, doesn't it?" His voice was patient.

"Can you imagine a girl going home stark naked except for a pair of shoes?"

"It's not that," said Brentford. "It's not where she was going, since we know that now, but why, and if you like, with whom. And it seems to me conclusive."

"That she was strangled here, before she got there?"

"What I was thinking was that if a girl were naked and alone, she would be going home.... But if she were naked and with someone, she'd have stopped when they came to that junction of the paths. They would have turned back, or gone the other way. No man would calmly take her home in that state."

Crosston stood among the bushes looking at the sandal among the tree roots. It had been wrenched off, it seemed, since the strap was broken. It was very tangible.

But he thought of Brentford's reasoning. He said: "No, I suppose ... No man except her father."

Brentford and Ball kept poker faces, grimly.

"And he wouldn't be calm," said Crosston.

"With a woman!" said Ball. "With a woman, if someone had met her wandering in the woods, she would have come as far as this."

"A woman would have lent her something to put on," said Brentford. "At least she would have expected it."

But Ball fought. It was not only that he wished to do so, to disprove everything that Brentford said knowingly and that Crosston said unknowing. It was his duty. You had to be right, he thought. You couldn't go up to a man, any more, and accuse him, or even start to question him, with an assumption of his guilt, on assumptions only.

Even if the assumptions had been dragged unwillingly and at last, in the form of statements and allegations that were virtually hearsay evidence of guilt, from a man who did not want to make them.

"Even if she got as far as this alone," said Ball. "What do you suggest we know? Only that the most likely probability is that she met someone coming the other way."

"Was anyone coming the other way?" Crosston looked at Brentford.

Brentford looked at the path.

Crosston shook his head: "You could prove anything from that."

"Then the Trueman-Davies's were at home. So were the Morris's. Feltham says he was, and the only people who could be coming down this path were the father or the mother."

"Or both, or Feltham," said Ball.

"Yes," said Brentford. "Either or both or Feltham." But he moved impatiently, not willingly but to get it over, and turned towards the Silcrests'.

"So Feltham's your man," said Crosston.

Brentford looked at him and shook his head, but only waited a moment to see Crosston's expression change.

Ball knew it was his duty now to act as a one-party opposition. He would now, until the last.

As they walked down the path and saw the bushes thinning ahead of them as they neared the Silcrest garden, he said: "The only indication we have that it was the father, and not the mother, is the story of a man who is virtually the mother's lover, and his only real evidence is hearsay, and what he says the mother herself has said."

Brentford was walking ahead of Ball along the path, and Ball had addressed the words to his back.

So he turned, looked at Ball and nodded, and then went on.

"And the only evidence we will have that it was the mother is what the father will say. And it's that we will have to contend with," he said. "That we know it in advance, this time."

Ball thought: and choose? Arrest one, and not the other, with certainty and virtually on sight, contending with the problem family of the Trequayne estate, not daring to make a mistake, when their intimates had failed?

That was their police task now.

CHAPTER THIRTY-FIVE

The Silcrest house, Brentford saw as they emerged from the woodland into the garden, was more traditional than the other houses on the estate. It had a careful, slightly mean, old-fashioned look, despite gables and ample chimneys, and it was partly overhung by trees.

Brentford wondered if there was anything in the presumption that a house echoed its owner's personality, and he looked at the dark blue front door, at the top of a flight of three steps, that was emphasised by a neat lintel and two artificial pillars.

The door was slowly opening.

It was not very surprising. They had been in view and coming across the garden for a little time, past flowerbeds that had an untidy appearance not seen at the other houses, and grass that needed to be cut and that was mixed with weeds.

The Silcrests must have been expecting them, not having been visited by the police since early in the day.

It was George Silcrest who came out. His clothes were covered with blood, they saw.

Brentford walked more quickly, while Ball began to run.

George Silcrest stood watching them. Apart from splashes of blood on his face and bald head, Brentford saw he was holding something in his right hand. It proved to be a razor.

I have overdone it, Brentford thought. Been too careful, considerate and delicate.

Anyone could say that delicacy was out of place in a case of murder, assuming they knew who the murderer was.

He watched Ball confronting the blood-soaked man. He did not hurry to Ball's aid. When there would be two of them in a moment, Ball would be foolish to indulge in heroics of any kind.

"Now give me that, sir," Ball said.

Silcrest handed him the razor meekly and without a word. Only then he said: "Suicide."

He looked a mediocre, uninspiring man, Brentford though. But so did Crippen.

Silcrest turned to Brentford and indicated the razor that Ball held. He said: "I had to break the bathroom door down to take it from her."

Even at that point, Brentford had a sinking feeling. He thought of Silcrest's ingenuity, and wondered if he knew.

Gravely, arriving, he said: "You look in a state, Mr. Silcrest. Do you mean your wife?"

Silcrest looked at him with the appealing eyes of misery.

"In the bathroom," he said.

So they trooped upstairs.

The Silcrest house had a square, Victorian hall, stairs, a hat-stand, and several white doors. But no one had to lead them. The blood on the stair carpet was a sufficient indication.

There were several of that kind of murder, Brentford knew, murders or cover-up murders that almost anyone with care could get away with. To have a boating accident with someone who could not swim was one of them, and another, simplest of all, was to cut a throat and say that, seeing the attempted suicide, you tried to take the razor.

Most murders were too complicated. The successful mur-dered introduced no complications at all, and even if he talked in his sleep, you could not prove it.

Silcrest spoke with the right degree of incoherence: "I heard a scream!"

Brentford saw that there were two doors open on the higher floor, and blood on both floors, inside the doors.

Silcrest, whom they had allowed to get to the front, stopped and seemed most interested in the bathroom.

Brentford looked at the damaged, sagging door, and pushed it open.

Helen Silcrest's naked, blood-smeared body lay on the floor. It did not look alive, for it was lying in a lake of blood.

All the same, Brentford decided to find out. He reached into the bathroom and hooked a towel off the towel rail, to drop on the floor to make an island. He stepped in on that.

Silcrest stood outside the door watching. Ball had gone on to the bedroom. From there he called, "This boy is dead!"

So was Helen Silcrest, Brentford saw. The wide gash on her throat had stopped bleeding, and her eyes were open.

Now, he thought, they must call Crosston, Crawford, and the murder squad, and start again. He stayed where he was and looked around.

"Is Mr. Silcrest all right, sir?" said Ball meaningfully from the doorway. "Shall I go to phone?"

Brentford looked. There was a dressing-gown with blood down the front hanging behind the door of the cylinder cupboard. The bath was dry. No water had been run in it. The bloodspots on it had run, but not spread.

He tried to calculate that the woman had taken off the dressing-gown before she had run the water. It did not work. It was the wrong order in which to have a bath.

It was only that people didn't.

He went out and looked at Silcrest, and Ball went down the stairs.

"I am sorry, sir," he said to Silcrest. "We will have to ask you more questions about your wife's suicide, but would you like to go to your room and change?"

Only it was no good, Brentford suddenly saw. They had been wrong about Silcrest, though his wife and not he, if the dry-bath meant anything, had been the murderer.

In one way it was too late for guesswork, Brentford saw, and in another it had ceased to be important.

For though Silcrest had seemed collected and sane when they had come to him, the second sight of Helen Silcrest had had a bad effect.

He had sunk to a squatting position on the landing, and was looking dazed and making babbling noises like a child.

Like a small child, Brentford thought, that had tried too hard and failed. Only they were not sensible noises, such as a child would make, to the accompaniment of its tears.

THE PERENNIAL LIBRARY MYSTERY SERIES

Delano Ames

CORPSE DIPLOMATIQUE   P 637, $2.84
"Sprightly and intelligent."

—New York Herald Tribune Book Review

FOR OLD CRIME'S SAKE   P 629, $2.84

MURDER, MAESTRO, PLEASE   P 630, $2.84
"If there is a more engaging couple in modern fiction than Jane and
Dagobert Brown, we have not met them."   *—Scotsman*

SHE SHALL HAVE MURDER   P 638, $2.84
"Combines the merit of both the English and American schools in the
new mystery. It's as breezy as the best of the American ones, and has
the sophistication and wit of any top-notch Britisher."

—New York Herald Tribune Book Review

E. C. Bentley

TRENT'S LAST CASE   P 440, $2.50
"One of the three best detective stories ever written."

—Agatha Christie

TRENT'S OWN CASE   P 516, $2.25
"I won't waste time saying that the plot is sound and the detection
satisfying. Trent has not altered a scrap and reappears with all his old
humor and charm."   —Dorothy L. Sayers

Gavin Black

A DRAGON FOR CHRISTMAS   P 473, $1.95
"Potent excitement!"   *—New York Herald Tribune*

THE EYES AROUND ME   P 485, $1.95
"I stayed up until all hours last night reading *The Eyes Around Me*,
which is something I do not do very often, but I was so intrigued by the
ingeniousness of Mr. Black's plotting and the witty way in which he spins
his mystery. I can only say that I enjoyed the book enormously."

—F. van Wyck Mason

YOU WANT TO DIE, JOHNNY?   P 472, $1.95
"Gavin Black doesn't just develop a pressure plot in suspense, he adds
uninfected wit, character, charm, and sharp knowledge of the Far East
to make rereading as keen as the first race-through."   *—Book Week*

THOU SHELL OF DEATH P 428, $1.95
"It has all the virtues of culture, intelligence and sensibility that the most exacting connoisseur could ask of detective fiction."
—*The Times* [London] *Literary Supplement*

THE WIDOW'S CRUISE P 399, $2.25
"A stirring suspense. . . . The thrilling tale leaves nothing to be desired."
—*Springfield Republican*

THE WORM OF DEATH P 400, $2.25
"It [The Worm of Death] is one of Blake's very best—and his best is better than almost anyone's." —Louis Untermeyer

John & Emery Bonett

A BANNER FOR PEGASUS P 554, $2.40
"A gem! Beautifully plotted and set. . . . Not only is the murder adroit and deserved, and the detection competent, but the love story is charming." —Jacques Barzun and Wendell Hertig Taylor

DEAD LION P 563, $2.40
"A clever plot, authentic background and interesting characters highly recommended this one." —*New Republic*

Christianna Brand

GREEN FOR DANGER P 551, $2.50
"You have to reach for the greatest of Great Names (Christie, Carr, Queen . . .) to find Brand's rivals in the devious subtleties of the trade."
—Anthony Boucher

TOUR DE FORCE P 572, $2.40
"Complete with traps for the over-ingenious, a double-reverse surprise ending and a key clue planted so fairly and obviously that you completely overlook it. If that's your idea of perfect entertainment, then seize at once upon *Tour de Force.*" —Anthony Boucher, *The New York Times*

James Byrom

OR BE HE DEAD P 585, $2.84
"A very original tale . . . Well written and steadily entertaining."
—Jacques Barzun & Wendell Hertig Taylor, *A Catalogue of Crime*

Henry Calvin

IT'S DIFFERENT ABROAD   P 640, $2.84
"What is remarkable and delightful, Mr. Calvin imparts a flavor of satire to what he renovates and compels us to take straight."

—Jacques Barzun

Marjorie Carleton

VANISHED   P 559, $2.40
"Exceptional . . . a minor triumph."
—Jacques Barzun and Wendell Hertig Taylor, *A Catalogue of Crime*

George Harmon Coxe

MURDER WITH PICTURES   P 527, $2.25
"[Coxe] has hit the bull's-eye with his first shot."

—*The New York Times*

Edmund Crispin

BURIED FOR PLEASURE   P 506, $2.50
"Absolute and unalloyed delight."

—Anthony Boucher, *The New York Times*

Lionel Davidson

THE MENORAH MEN   P 592, $2.84
"Of his fellow thriller writers, only John Le Carré shows the same instinct for the viscera."   —*Chicago Tribune*

NIGHT OF WENCESLAS   P 595, $2.84
"A most ingenious thriller, so enriched with style, wit, and a sense of serious comedy that it all but transcends its kind."

—*The New Yorker*

THE ROSE OF TIBET   P 593, $2.84
"I hadn't realized how much I missed the genuine Adventure story . . . until I read *The Rose of Tibet*."   —Graham Greene

D. M. Devine

MY BROTHER'S KILLER   P 558, $2.40
"A most enjoyable crime story which I enjoyed reading down to the last moment."   —Agatha Christie

Kenneth Fearing

THE BIG CLOCK   P 500, $1.95
"It will be some time before chill-hungry clients meet again so rare a compound of irony, satire, and icy-fingered narrative. *The Big Clock* is . . . a psychothriller you won't put down."   —*Weekly Book Review*

Andrew Garve

THE ASHES OF LODA   P 430, $1.50
"Garve . . . embellishes a fine fast adventure story with a more credible picture of the U.S.S.R. than is offered in most thrillers."
         —*The New York Times Book Review*

THE CUCKOO LINE AFFAIR   P 451, $1.95
". . . an agreeable and ingenious piece of work."   —*The New Yorker*

A HERO FOR LEANDA   P 429, $1.50
"One can trust Mr. Garve to put a fresh twist to any situation, and the ending is really a lovely surprise."   —*The Manchester Guardian*

MURDER THROUGH THE LOOKING GLASS   P 449, $1.95
". . . refreshingly out-of-the-way and enjoyable . . . highly recommended to all comers."   —*Saturday Review*

NO TEARS FOR HILDA   P 441, $1.95
"It starts fine and finishes finer. I got behind on breathing watching Max get not only his man but his woman, too."   —Rex Stout

THE RIDDLE OF SAMSON   P 450, $1.95
"The story is an excellent one, the people are quite likable, and the writing is superior."   —*Springfield Republican*

Michael Gilbert

BLOOD AND JUDGMENT   P 446, $1.95
"Gilbert readers need scarcely be told that the characters all come alive at first sight, and that his surpassing talent for narration enhances any plot. . . . Don't miss."   —*San Francisco Chronicle*

THE BODY OF A GIRL   P 459, $1.95
"Does what a good mystery should do: open up into all kinds of ramifications, with untold menace behind the action. At the end, there is a bang-up climax, and it is a pleasure to see how skilfully Gilbert wraps everything up."   —*The New York Times Book Review*

THE DANGER WITHIN   P 448, $1.95
"Michael Gilbert has nicely combined some elements of the straight
detective story with plenty of action, suspense, and adventure, to produce a superior thriller."   —*Saturday Review*

FEAR TO TREAD   P 458, $1.95
"Merits serious consideration as a work of art."
                                        —*The New York Times*

Joe Gores

HAMMETT   P 631, $2.84
"Joe Gores at his very best. Terse, powerful writing—with the master,
Dashiell Hammett, as the protagonist in a novel I think he would have
been proud to call his own."   —Robert Ludlum

C. W. Grafton

BEYOND A REASONABLE DOUBT   P 519, $1.95
"A very ingenious tale of murder . . . a brilliant and gripping narrative."
                        —Jacques Barzun and Wendell Hertig Taylor

THE RAT BEGAN TO GNAW THE ROPE   P 639, $2.84
"Fast, humorous story with flashes of brilliance."
                                        —*The New Yorker*

Edward Grierson

THE SECOND MAN   P 528, $2.25
"One of the best trial-testimony books to have come along in quite a
while."   —*The New Yorker*

Bruce Hamilton

TOO MUCH OF WATER   P 635, $2.84
"A superb sea mystery. . . . The prose is excellent."
        —Jacques Barzun and Wendell Hertig Taylor, *A Catalogue of Crime*

Cyril Hare

DEATH IS NO SPORTSMAN   P 555, $2.40
"You will be thrilled because it succeeds in placing an ingenious story
in a new and refreshing setting. . . . The identity of the murderer is really
a surprise."   —*Daily Mirror*

Cyril Hare (cont'd)

DEATH WALKS THE WOODS   P 556, $2.40

"Here is a fine formal detective story, with a technically brilliant solution demanding the attention of all connoisseurs of construction."

— Anthony Boucher, *The New York Times Book Review*

AN ENGLISH MURDER   P 455, $2.50

"By a long shot, the best crime story I have read for a long time. Everything is traditional, but originality does not suffer. The setting is perfect. Full marks to Mr. Hare."   *—Irish Press*

SUICIDE EXCEPTED   P 636, $2.84

"Adroit in its manipulation . . . and distinguished by a plot-twister which I'll wager Christie wishes she'd thought of."

—The New York Times

TENANT FOR DEATH   P 570, $2.84

"The way in which an air of probability is combined both with clear, terse narrative and with a good deal of subtle suburban atmosphere, proves the extreme skill of the writer."   *—The Spectator*

TRAGEDY AT LAW   P 522, $2.25

"An extremely urbane and well-written detective story."

—The New York Times

UNTIMELY DEATH   P 514, $2.25

"The English detective story at its quiet best, meticulously underplayed, rich in perceivings of the droll human animal and ready at the last with a neat surprise which has been there all the while had we but wits to see it."   *—New York Herald Tribune Book Review*

THE WIND BLOWS DEATH   P 589, $2.84

"A plot compounded of musical knowledge, a Dickens allusion, and a subtle point in law is related with delightfully unobtrusive wit, warmth, and style."   *—The New York Times*

WITH A BARE BODKIN   P 523, $2.25

"One of the best detective stories published for a long time."

—The Spectator

Robert Harling

THE ENORMOUS SHADOW   P 545, $2.50

"In some ways the best spy story of the modern period. . . . The writing is terse and vivid . . . the ending full of action . . . altogether first-rate."

— Jacques Barzun and Wendell Hertig Taylor, *A Catalogue of Crime*

Matthew Head

THE CABINDA AFFAIR   P 541, $2.25
"An absorbing whodunit and a distinguished novel of atmosphere."
—Anthony Boucher, *The New York Times*

THE CONGO VENUS   P 597, $2.84
"Terrific. The dialogue is just plain wonderful."
—*The Boston Globe*

MURDER AT THE FLEA CLUB   P 542, $2.50
"The true delight is in Head's style, its limpid ease combined with humor
and an awesome precision of phrase."   —*San Francisco Chronicle*

M. V. Heberden

ENGAGED TO MURDER   P 533, $2.25
"Smooth plotting."   —*The New York Times*

James Hilton

WAS IT MURDER?   P 501, $1.95
"The story is well planned and well written."
—*The New York Times*

P. M. Hubbard

HIGH TIDE   P 571, $2.40
"A smooth elaboration of mounting horror and danger."
—*Library Journal*

Elspeth Huxley

THE AFRICAN POISON MURDERS   P 540, $2.25
"Obscure venom, manical mutilations, deadly bush fire, thrilling climax
compose major opus.... Top-flight."
—*Saturday Review of Literature*

MURDER ON SAFARI   P 587, $2.84
"Right now we'd call Mrs. Huxley a dangerous rival to Agatha Christie."   —*Books*

Francis Iles

BEFORE THE FACT   P 517, $2.50
"Not many 'serious' novelists have produced character studies to compare with Iles's internally terrifying portrait of the murderer in *Before the Fact,* his masterpiece and a work truly deserving the appellation of unique and beyond price."   —Howard Haycraft

MALICE AFORETHOUGHT   P 532, $1.95
"It is a long time since I have read anything so good as *Malice Afore-thought,* with its cynical humour, acute criminology, plausible detail and rapid movement. It makes you hug yourself with pleasure."
                                      —H. C. Harwood, *Saturday Review*

Michael Innes

THE CASE OF THE JOURNEYING BOY   P 632, $3.12
"I could see no faults in it. There is no one to compare with him."
                                      —*Illustrated London News*

DEATH BY WATER   P 574, $2.40
"The amount of ironic social criticism and deft characterization of scenes and people would serve another author for six books."
                                      —Jacques Barzun and Wendell Hertig Taylor

HARE SITTING UP   P 590, $2.84
"There is hardly anyone (in mysteries or mainstream) more exquisitely literate, allusive and Jamesian—and hardly anyone with a firmer sense of melodramatic plot or a more vigorous gift of storytelling."
                                      —Anthony Boucher, *The New York Times*

THE LONG FAREWELL   P 575, $2.40
"A model of the deft, classic detective story, told in the most wittily diverting prose."   —*The New York Times*

THE MAN FROM THE SEA   P 591, $2.84
"The pace is brisk, the adventures exciting and excitingly told, and above all he keeps to the very end the interesting ambiguity of the man from the sea."   —*New Statesman*

THE SECRET VANGUARD   P 584, $2.84
"Innes . . . has mastered the art of swift, exciting and well-organized narrative."   —*The New York Times*

THE WEIGHT OF THE EVIDENCE   P 633, $2.84
"First-class puzzle, deftly solved. University background interesting and amusing."   —*Saturday Review of Literature*

Mary Kelly

THE SPOILT KILL   P 565, $2.40
"Mary Kelly is a new Dorothy Sayers. . . . [An] exciting new novel."
                                                    —*Evening News*

Lange Lewis

THE BIRTHDAY MURDER   P 518, $1.95
"Almost perfect in its playlike purity and delightful prose."
                              —Jacques Barzun and Wendell Hertig Taylor

Allan MacKinnon

HOUSE OF DARKNESS   P 582, $2.84
"His best . . . a perfect compendium."
   —Jacques Barzun & Wendell Hertig Taylor, *A Catalogue of Crime*

Arthur Maling

LUCKY DEVIL   P 482, $1.95
"The plot unravels at a fast clip, the writing is breezy and Maling's
approach is as fresh as today's stockmarket quotes."
                                         —*Louisville Courier Journal*

RIPOFF   P 483, $1.95
"A swiftly paced story of today's big business is larded with intrigue as
a Ralph Nader-type investigates an insurance scandal and is soon on the
run from a hired gun and his brother. . . . Engrossing and credible."
                                                          —*Booklist*

SCHROEDER'S GAME   P 484, $1.95
"As the title indicates, this Schroeder is up to something, and the un-
ravelling of his game is a diverting and sufficiently blood-soaked entertainment."   —*The New Yorker*

Austin Ripley

MINUTE MYSTERIES   P 387, $2.50
More than one hundred of the world's shortest detective stories. Only
one possible solution to each case!

Thomas Sterling

THE EVIL OF THE DAY   P 529, $2.50
"Prose as witty and subtle as it is sharp and clear. . .characters unconven-
tionally conceived and richly bodied forth . . . . In short, a novel to be
treasured."   —Anthony Boucher, *The New York Times*

Julian Symons

THE BELTING INHERITANCE   P 468, $1.95
"A superb whodunit in the best tradition of the detective story."
                              —August Derleth, *Madison Capital Times*

BLAND BEGINNING   P 469, $1.95
"Mr. Symons displays a deft storytelling skill, a quiet and literate wit,
a nice feeling for character, and detectival ingenuity of a high order."
                              —Anthony Boucher, *The New York Times*

BOGUE'S FORTUNE   P 481, $1.95
"There's a touch of the old sardonic humour, and more than a touch of
style."   —*The Spectator*

THE BROKEN PENNY   P 480, $1.95
"The most exciting, astonishing and believable spy story to appear in
years.   —Anthony Boucher, *The New York Times Book Review*

THE COLOR OF MURDER   P 461, $1.95
"A singularly unostentatious and memorably brilliant detective story."
                              —*New York Herald Tribune Book Review*

Dorothy Stockbridge Tillet
(John Stephen Strange)

THE MAN WHO KILLED FORTESCUE   P 536, $2.25
"Better than average."   —*Saturday Review of Literature*

Simon Troy

THE ROAD TO RHUINE   P 583, $2.84
"Unusual and agreeably told."   —*San Francisco Chronicle*

SWIFT TO ITS CLOSE   P 546, $2.40
"A nicely literate British mystery . . . the atmosphere and the plot are
exceptionally well wrought, the dialogue excellent."   —*Best Sellers*

Henry Wade

THE DUKE OF YORK'S STEPS   P 588, $2.84
"A classic of the golden age."
   —Jacques Barzun & Wendell Hertig Taylor, *A Catalogue of Crime*

A DYING FALL   P 543, $2.50
"One of those expert British suspense jobs . . . it crackles with undercur-
rents of blackmail, violent passion and murder. Topnotch in its class."
                                              —*Time*

If you enjoyed this book you'll want to know about
THE PERENNIAL LIBRARY MYSTERY SERIES

Buy them at your local bookstore or use this coupon for ordering:

Qty	P number	Price

postage and handling charge	$1.00
_____ book(s) @ $0.25	
TOTAL	

Prices contained in this coupon are Harper & Row invoice prices only. They are subject to change without notice, and in no way reflect the prices at which these books may be sold by other suppliers.

HARPER & ROW, Mail Order Dept. #PMS, 10 East 53rd St., New York, N.Y. 10022.

Please send me the books I have checked above. I am enclosing $_____ which includes a postage and handling charge of $1.00 for the first book and 25¢ for each additional book. Send check or money order. No cash or C.O.D.s please

Name_____

Address_____

City_____ State_____ Zip_____

Please allow 4 weeks for delivery. USA only. This offer expires 11/30/84. Please add applicable sales tax.